Castletown

By P. Symonds

TSL Publications

First published in Great Britain in 2020
By TSL Publications, Rickmansworth

Copyright © 2020 Paul Symonloe

ISBN / 978-1-913294-26-7

DEDICATION

to my beautiful boys

Castletown

A tale in sixteen majestic chunks

Chunk One.

Opening Shots

I sat in my bedsit bathroom defecating pleasurably, looking out at Castletown. This early Sunday the good and irritating folk of that settlement were mostly still asleep under duvets, or sleepily satisfying one or other appetite in their largely agreeable lives. In one bedroom (of five) their *gentleman's family* (one boy and one girl) were left to a Polish au pair, while their parents used the opportunity for a *quickie* in a brief oasis away from the work-desert. Ah! (They told themselves) *doggy-style ... because I'm worth it!* I continued my long evacuation, taking in with interest the gunmetal-grey of Castletown Castle. I wondered casually if perhaps the *Royal* was also submitting to this imperative of nature, and was unloading with me in synchronised dumping. Was she? No matter. What's important here are the simple facts; call them facts of life, or if you like, the facts of the town. What it comes down to is that any town, in this case Castletown, is a seething, irrational, imperfect and thus normal kind of place. It was a small town. Its thinking was small; it exhibited small-town hypocrisy, pomposity and small minds. Its townsfolk almost certainly had small genitalia. What, I asked myself, *is* Castletown? Is it like all towns in England but with *knobs on,* and in? Does it exhibit all the customary human weaknesses; the inability to be or do anything that isn't self-interested and literal-minded? Is it inhabited by those whose seemingly sole aim is to belong to some actual or theoretical club? Is it for those of us who just want to belong; to be part of the fearful mass – agreeing to agree? Is Castletown this?

🏰 🏰 🏰

I headed out to see for myself; treading the narrow old streets that led to wider old streets and the new-*olde* shops. These new *olde shoppes* reassured modern minds that sound *olde-fashionede* values survived to the modern day.

On the streets were the modern-medieval minds and the primitive-modern doings of the 21st century fortress. I already knew I didn't belong here. In fact, I didn't even *begin* to belong to Castletown. I was a graft – an attachment. I just couldn't get *into* the town. Behind a membrane I looked on, observing. I came to Castletown seeking independence from my parents and a distance from *home.* The problem was (my parents told me and it was probably true) that I'd crossed too many lines; overstepped too many marks; put too many backs up and burned too many boats. There was little I could do about any of this now, so I simply carried on observing. Though revealing this was like looking through the wrong end of a telescope. Things were there but out of reach. I could judge them, weigh them up, but not *feel* them. I felt *durexed* against full sensitivity. My detachment however meant I could see things not clear to those souls inside the movie screen, *living* their story. These beings were trapped by their parts inside the screen. These thought-words, *trapped by their parts,* lingered in my mind as I passed the tattooist's parlour and the hamburger outlet. In this last sat a muscle-bound man wearing a look of brutal simplicity. His loudly dressed *partner* sat opposite, shouting at two shaven headed kids fighting over a burger. Their small eyes looked around, making sure while staring through the pane, their mouths were supplied with burger. Adapted as they were to the 21st century, these kids were divided only by time rather than type from their predecessors of eight or nine hundred years. These were very much the same urchins of this same town of the 9th or 10th centuries. While William the Conqueror was busy knocking up castles, these kids were running around the ground-works making a nuisance of themselves. A kind of genetic time-travel had propelled them from the Dark Ages to the Digital Age. I had to say they looked remarkably unmoved by the experience. In the *here and now* they were doing mostly the same things as their forbears, the only difference being that today's burgers had replaced greasy chicken wings. The shaven kids continued to gorge, while the parents maintained vague satiated stares across and beyond each other. They made occasional bored conversation, stopping every so often to curse at each other, or at one, or both, of their offspring. Life went on as normal, while outside the traffic inched over the *sleeping police-man/men/persons* (whichever it is) on the boutique-riddled streets of Castle-town. I wondered if the Royal had wakened and was peradventure, at this very minute, taking a lightly buttered breakfast in some silvery antechamber off one of the castle's labyrinthine passages.

My personal labyrinthine passage was, given the time of day, beginning to make hunger-music along the lines of haunting whale-song, though less attractive. I decided (in *snack-speak*) on a *lite bite* at a local café-bar to address the situation. I knew one in an Italianate style which Americans (*Italianate Americans indeed*) attempt for continental cafés. These had mushroomed all over England in recent years. On the positive side I considered, you can at almost any hour of the day buy:

    A bucket of foul brown liquid,

    A larger bucket of evil looking liquid,

    A bath-full of nauseating brown liquid with a *head* on it.

This *head* is what remains of the cleaning agent used religiously to clean the machine that dispenses it, combined with the after-taste of the gooey metal spike that heats it, and froths it up with a loud whooshing noise. Inside mock-animated waiting staff (latterly, mysteriously called *baristas*) sometimes spoke enough English to understand you, but if they didn't, insinuated it was your fault. They were zealously over-trained in vigorously cleaning the coffee making machinery. Old-fashioned considerations like listening to your order and getting it right; clearing tables etc. went out of the window. Inside the window, and inside the kitchen, was a hopeful-looking friend of a friend over from Poland trying to shag an English girl. On the gastronomic side of things, today I was determined to make a more agreeable choice than the brown fluid. I chose a flavoured water tasting of Aspartame and a chunky prefabricated Italianate biscuit sealed in a vindictively unopenable cellophane packet. This was priced at five times its value, still it was my choice! I had quite decided on sitting in the mock Italian interior and listening to Castletown folk discussing their lives; confiding in each other about their marriages, jobs, plans etc. One woman was saying to another:

"I turns round to 'im and says listen you, I'm 'effing not 'aving it no more! You get it!?"

Why, I thought, do people have to *turn round* so much in conversations? They seemed to be in a dizzyingly permanent state of rotation. At another table was an older couple with silvering hair and expensively-made raincoats, looking impassively across at each other. The woman spoke softly, while her husband bore a look of much-practiced agreement.

"I've *always told Graeme* he lacks brains, and if one lacks brains it's best to just look extremely serious and say nothing."

Her husband nodded faithfully.

Again, I scanned the interior of the Italianate café. A couple of *mates* were discussing an upcoming stag weekend in Barcelona. I guessed they were twenty-two or twenty-three. The first *mate* was dressed in drainpipe jeans and a T-shirt with *Led Zeppelin* on a black background, while the other was in working clothes, replete with paint spatter, so I guessed this was his lunch-break.

"The place we need to go is called the *Ramblas*."

Paint Mate was explaining.

11

"It's wall to wall snatch."

Led Zeppelin Mate grinned.

"That's where the action is right?"

"Yeah! There's loads of cool places in the city. It's going to be a frigging blast mate!"

"Look Steve how much dough are you takin'? Are you earning at the minute or what?"

It appeared *Paint Mate* had a name.

"I reckon £200 should do it. Why, aren't you earning?"

Led Zeppelin Mate looked glum.

"Nah, Mike had to lose me didn't he? I was wondering if you could loan me a *ton*?"

Paint Mate considered.

"Can't your old lady stump up some dosh?"

Paint Mate (being of Irish extraction, meant his friend's mother here rather than a girlfriend or wife.)

"Fuck no! She's still working 'er way up to zero tolerance!"

The conversation turned to negotiating the finer terms of the loan and I lost interest for a while.

The comings and goings continued in the Italianate café-bar, conceived by an Italianate American, possibly from California. I could see things were hotting up now with lunchtime punters ordering paninis and café lattes. Some *suits* were talking in loud assertive voices about *deals* and *closing*. I sipped at my Aspartame with flavouring. Two tall twenty*whatever*-year olds were talking about *Ian* and how he was a *real wanker* because promotion *always* went to *bloody graduates*, like him, rather than honest *work your way up from the ground floor guys,* presumably like them. They would though, I thought, both instantly trade places with *Ian the Wanker* in a heartbeat given half a chance.

Meanwhile in the Italianate café I turned to watch two unmarried or separated *singlemums* (one word). One was going *on and on* about how she wasn't getting her *support* through, but how *supportive* her girl-friends had been since *it* happened. The other apparently had been through *absolute shit too*, since *that bastard* had *buggered off* with *her, the bitch,* and how now she spent *so much time* with her girl-friends 'cause women *understand each other, don't they*? And, *all men are bastards*, and that she *knows* that Ryan and Jason will grow up to *totally respect women yeah*? They won't. But, *that bloke who came round to put up the shed was really tasty* and she *wouldn't mind getting her hands on 'is nice little arse* would she? The second woman, with a pinched nose and tight pair of *up both cracks* leggings and a denim top, said that *she had always been through loads of shit with blokes* who (again) *were all bastards,* and made hand movements to make it clear they spent most of their time in *one to one meetings* with their genitalia. Also that (meaning the *meetings* thing) along with beer and football, was all that blokes did! The first woman nodded vigorously and leaned forward.

"Yeah, but 'ave their uses!"

She measured six or seven inches between her hands, letting out a laugh-scream. As one, they looked around grinning to see if anyone had heard, to be rewarded by a shocked look on the face of a mild, conventional-looking woman somewhere in her fifties. With this the *singlemums* appeared content, and looked away engaged with their own thoughts.

This short lull allowed me a moment of observation time for a couple of (it seemed at first) lawyer types who had just launched themselves into the café, suggesting in their movements and voices, they considered themselves above other, run-of-the-mill, punters. They were getting ready to hold forth (it seemed to me) in very loud voices about largely themselves, but possibly also about other matters, so I waited. The larger and taller of the suits was also louder than his squatter sidekick, and wore a very pale grey suit. He wore his hair swept back Michael Douglas style, and his (now I thought actually quite stumpy) side-kick, while still loud, had a rather nasal delivery, turning his entire side of the conversation into commentary as though spoken through a cardboard tube. *Tall One* said did he (*Stumpy*) realise in fact that he (*Tall One*) had *masterminded a new initiative in the area of universal consumables* and then leered pointedly at Stumpy for some kind of recognition. Stumpy duly nodded sagely and returned that *it was clear the foreign initiative had been a real wake up call for those useless wankers in Dusseldorf. Tall One* looked gratified and gave *Stumpy* a reassuring look as though to encourage him in some self-congratulation of his own, if only to a suitably, carefully calibrated, lesser degree, because he was, after all, a lesser being.

"*I* was, *of course* (*Stumpy*'s nasal drawl), the only person in any kind of senior position, *in any way shape or form.*"

He dwelt lovingly over each word as though they had been hand-tooled in precious metal.

Who had any idea, *at all* (he emphasised this with a fist on an open palm) *that this whole north-south thing was about to break.*

He looked up at *Tall One* hoping that much approval would follow. *Tall One* stopped and pondered almost endlessly in thought and then, as if pulling a rabbit out of a hat, bestowed a sudden reassuring smile-leer on *Stumpy*. The latter relaxed visibly and allowed himself an internal smile, mentally chalking up a point. Mild interest gave way to boredom as *Tall One* and *Stumpy* gave each other more of the same ego-massaging routine and veered off into the demerits (by comparison with themselves) of the *Lille Office* and the *Teddington Tossers* who should have been *downsized when fucking Barry retired* and probably also *shot for good measure.*

I turned back to the exchanges between *Paint Mate* and *Led Zeppelin Mate* which had reached a successful outcome by the sound of it.

"Thanks mate, you're one in a million!"

"Nah, it's okay so long as I get it back by the end of the month, right?"

"Yeah no probs, you're like a brother to me you know that?"

"Don't worry about it. I'd do it for any mate."

"Yeah but for me it's like we're family. I bet we'll go to each other's funerals."

Paint Mate stared at him wonderingly.

"Yeah right ..."

Now I was at a decision point. Did I go back to work or wander through the shady mini-passages of old Castletown's cobbled streets. The latter was a good idea, I persuaded myself, since this afternoon was the first sun we had seen in a summer of floods and almost eternal glowering cloudy, windy, raining bastard weather. So off I went to view the good and industrious folk of Castletown and inspect the grazing tourist throngs, themselves rather like weather systems, coming up from the station and the coach parks in ragged troughs of ample and loudly dressed jollity.

Chunk Two.

Bafflements

I looked up and observed Castletown Castle towering over me doing its imperious, detached routine. It looked on, gave nothing away, offered no clues to the insect-mortals crawling round its base whether something of significance was about to happen, or if life was just taking another standard heartbeat in the billions on its *watch*. The castle didn't *do* surprise. You are left feeling there must be more to hear and see, but the castle confounded you with a sense of imposing grey mystery. There were though, always gasps of surprise in store for the meandering tourist groups spreading and developing in mini *weather systems,* grazing their way up towards the statue of the dead royal. At the same time, mostly pleasant and reassuring surprise was imminent for those who strode the town in *I belong* mode. They were adding to their *standing* along with other like-minded stalwarts of the town. These local *characters* exchanged snippets of dialogue and nods of recognition. Sometimes only looks were traded; silent nods of understanding. Local *faces* sent each other mute messages of recognition and perceived status. They stretched their necks up involuntarily, echoing the movements of the mute swans on the river close by. I walked on through the charming lights and shades of the town, past the cafes, and the restaurants of the setting I'd made home. I wondered if the visitors and tourists to this town had taken in these revealing, unseen signals. I realised the silent signals of the townsfolk are not *snaps* you could take. These abstractions were easily, though, the most telling traits. Like wisps of smoke giving away secret fires smoldering in the hearts and minds of Castletown folk. Puzzling, perhaps, unless you were *in the know* ... The Castle knew, so too did the ancient, crazed cobbled-streets. If you wanted to know more though, you'd have to serve your time. Until then, the drawbridge was up, with you on the wrong side of the mote; remote.

The day was standing smartly to attention at 12 noon, ready for inspection. I was getting itchy to review other parts of Castletown that I knew. I wanted to get some knowledge of the modern-primordial people who we all are. This was my working day; to satisfy my fascination for the way people in Castletown conducted themselves as they did. I'd like to understand what they did and, if I could, why they thought their way was the *only way*. I conceded that I have little idea why some people do what they do, and in particular I was baffled by the rituals of the Castletowners. I especially wanted to know what they brought forward from their long-run origins in the town, and how they reconciled this with the modern world. I had learned one thing that really gets under people's skin is any challenge to their list of beliefs. Let's call this their *List*. Others having a different List from ours, and disagreeing with our List, really upsets us. It wasn't current at the time of this story, but I've since watched a TV *reality show* about wives and families swapping their lives and homes for those of another wife/family. Wife A (with *List*) moves into the home of a parallel wife and adopts her family. Wife B does the same. From this point, for an agreed period, they consent to live as replacements according to the other wife's List. No sex of course! Boy but (and it's sometimes a big *butt*) the faux wife and her *wifestyle* are ferocious! After a few scornful observations about the state of the *opponent* wife's house, her slovenly habits, and her *pig* husband, the wives engage in a bitching contest to the death. According to their respective Lists, wife A believes, *passionately,* in eating raw vegetables, while wife B believes equally passionately in an intravenous hamburger drip. I'm baffled by the absolutes. Where's the balance? Why does the green, seaweed munching, brown rice cooking, sandal-wearer hold such extreme beliefs? Surely liberal thinkers should be more liberal-minded? Why is the eating of an occasional hamburger equivalent to selling your children into white slavery? Is it not in itself slavery of the mind to be at either of these extremes? Equally the hamburger-gorger argues that she simply *must* eat fat. Anything else is a betrayal in favour of either *posh nosh* or *foreign muck*. Why no middle ground? This is surely the problem I thought, no lights and shades. This war, like most wars, is about territory, the territorial boundaries of their *lists*. Surely such food extremists are just as wrong as each other?

Bafflement reigned over my reflections as I picked my way through the back streets nearby the looming castle walls. Narrow alleys separated the close-hugging, ancient buildings. These latter leaned gently towards each other as though to prop each other up. They said: *come on old chap, just a few hundred years more!* Nevertheless mute and conspiratorial, they always made sure outsiders didn't see clean into their mysterious inner works. Tourists and others drifted past. A couple of children giggled to each other and lampooned their parents' lost sense of fun. I thought all the shops looked the same these days. Why aren't they all different and individual like they used to be? There was a time when shops had character. Now all you see are the same names offering the same generic products. If you hit your head while shopping and lost your memory I thought, you'd probably never find out which town you were in. That is if Castletown wasn't quite different and special, which of course it is! Here you'd find out where you were pretty quickly ... Now Slothtown ... up the road would be more of a challenge. I'd worked at Slothtown Cemetery (a summer job) not long before this story starts. Now that was an experience!

My job was tending the gardens and paving. I was one of a *Gang of Four* (as we came to call ourselves) young men fresh out of university and willing to do anything for ready cash to fund our social lives. At the time *cash* came in neat brown envelopes on Friday afternoons, ending each sinew-straining week. It was the moment we all worked towards, and for which we put up with boredom and blisters. On day one we were met by the elderly and highly zealous Crematorium Head Gardener brandishing a one-pronged hoe.

"*This* is your weapon of choice!" he suggested.

I guessed he was *actually* a war veteran and that holding the hoe like a bayonet was from real-life experience.

"This whole place (he stretched his arm impressively across the near horizon from east to west) *is alive with death!*"

This was enough to bond our Gang of Four together inseparably. It was a gift we couldn't have hoped for, and the humour and lampooning that stemmed from it carried us through the summer.

Carl (one of the Gang) wept with laughter every time we arrived in the morning, mimicking the Head Gardener's delivery.

"This place is alivvve with deathhhh!"

He accompanied this oath with a wild parody of stabbing at weeds lodged between the large grey paving slabs of the crematorium main drive (this is what the one pronged hoe was intended for) sometimes catching his ankles in his enthusiasm, and ending up writhing about on the ground in pain and mirth in equal measure.

The summer turned out to be fine and warm, and friendships were easily and naturally made. If the truth is told though, the story of the summer at Slothtown Cemetery is inserted here not to represent just a casual reminiscence of early adulthood and the camaraderie of chance friends. The fact is, that despite that fine and entertaining summer, I was actually quite depressed. I couldn't put my finger on when it had started but the clouds were certainly massed *over* me. The *Gang of Four* took me out of myself much of the time, but shadows awaited me as the end of the day approached. The pathological self-confidence of youth was displaced by a sense that I hadn't really achieved very much in life. This fact, contrasting starkly with my high-flying Oxbridge-educated brothers, weighed on me. Not that this was my only hang-up, but I latched onto it as a badge of shame. I want this chapter in my life known, so when we go on with our story, we have some background, a canvass. I realised it (the depression that is) had to be tackled, which is where Tom PA comes in. Tom PA ran a psychotherapy practice in West Acton from a musty Victorian house with lots of aging soft furniture. He also had a beautiful dark-eyed daughter called Diana. By the time of my first appointment, I had taken to riding a Honda C70 Moped, and threaded my way up the A40, past the Hoover building, and then on through the tight capillaries of West London. On arrival I parked in Tom's drive and pressed a round old-fashioned bell which sounded somewhere vaguely inside the house. It was Diana who let me in, asking me sweetly, but formally, my name and the time of my appointment. I fell in love with her immediately, and thinking of her made my visits easier. The sessions with Tom were nonetheless interesting of themselves. He asked me (I suppose he'd had Freudian training) to lie on a velveteen-covered chaise and relax. It was strange, to say the least, staring at the ornate ceiling-rose in the musty-smelling house telling Tom (a handsome well-built man of around forty, with Diana's dark eyes) what ailed me. At the same time it was strangely liberating and I told him everything. His voice came from above and beyond me (he was sitting in a chair a foot or two from the head of the chaise) strong and reassuring. The voice asked: "So you feel somehow inferior to your brothers?"

I stared at the ceiling-rose.

"I feel I haven't *done anything*, if you know what I mean?"

"And they *have*?"

"Oxbridge," I explained, intending the one word to support a solid weight of meaning.

I took it Tom was slightly amused from the small gurgle he made here.

"How old are you?"

"Twenty-two."

"And already you condemn yourself for not having *done much*?"

When he put it like this it did sound a little silly, but it *felt* bad, this was my point.

It took ten sessions with Tom PA, and ten brushes with his beautiful dark-eyed daughter to really convince me that life wasn't over. It was, I suppose, the angst of youth. It was nevertheless a very bad time, and ingrained in me never to underestimate the desperation sometimes felt by the young.

At Castletown Post Office the queue was *out of the door*. Needing to post a recorded delivery letter, I'd considered waiting for a quieter time, but decided in the end to stick it out. The long queue I reckoned was because the last seven days on God's earth had been a week of godawful weather and all the elderly folk and the *singlemums* had chosen this dry *window* to get a few things done. I waited with a show of patience and watched people in the queue. I was at a point in the queue nearest the counter, a kink in the human chain allowing me to observe those currently being served. I was alarmed to hear a kindly-looking old woman *settling in* for a proper conversation.

"Yes, *those* forms used to be *blue* but now they're *pink*."

"Oh yes, I remember that *too,* they *were* blue now you come to mention it."

I felt a wave of irritation. Be p*atient* I told myself; you can't rush people, especially at their age. Stay calm and let it happen. It's no big deal… After some fifteen minutes of *slug*-motion I might actually have made it. That is, had *Yosemite Sam* not stormed into my head, hopping on the spot like a tiny purple Harrier Jump-Jet. Bugger these ankle-high tittle-tattlers! We'd hardly moved! Why were they so happy to let the precious hours of life slip away? If these silvering pension-grabbers didn't stop comparing the colour of fucking forms I'd blow them all away with a sawn-off shot gun! For crissakes one colour had *ceased to be* and the other colour has been *introduced.* What blind bit of difference did it make? Perhaps we should call for a *third* opinion. Maybe we should canvass the whole sodding town to see if blue or pink was better! … No, no, I calmed down. These were simply innocent elderly people going about their day, interacting as regular human beings. I let the irritation die down, tension releasing like a valve on a pressure cooker. I carried on observing. A wide

23

ribbon of blue nylon somewhat contained the post office's clients, only bulging in parts where the Castletown old or young leaned on it, being oblivious or mischievous. Among those stretching the ribbon were a really very, very large man and an equally extremely large and *matching* woman. They stood solidly, like twin *islands* towards my end of the queue, speaking intermittently and slowly. They *issued* words with a certain ventriloquist-like projection (stemming, I guessed from the size of their diaphragms). I couldn't really see their lips moving. They had both decided at some point in life that certain clothes, haircuts and habits suited their vastness. They each wore open flapping coats with no detectable hems or fastenings, allowing for maximum freedom of movement. The *fattist* in the post office clientele was evident in the, studiously disinterested, sneaked looks around me. Unconsciously we looked ourselves up and down for inner reassurance that we had not *let ourselves go* like the Huge Ones. Yet, apparently, we're nearly all toting around dangerously high levels of *bad fat* on our trunks and arses. How apt we are to *think* in judgment of others, while outwardly squeaking inside the norms of acceptable behaviour. We keep inside the membrane; follow the rules, so long as the next man or woman does so. I guessed that such *rules* would crumble away like a bank of dry earth in a flood. If a biblical flood came today it would be every man or woman for themselves. So called civilized behaviour would evaporate in a heartbeat, like childhood chaos when the teacher leaves the classroom. Likewise, after a shipwreck, once you'd washed up on a beach somewhere and counted yourselves; as you're earnestly asking if everyone's still alive, *that's the moment* for sizing up your fellow man as your next square meal. So much for rules and laws! I had to admit to occasionally bending the rules, but I was personally determined never to actually *eat* my fellow man. I quietly approved of my little stamp of personal morality just as I finally came to the *business end* of the post office counter. Having dealt with my recorded delivery, I left the building to those gentle grey-haired citizens from an earlier era, debating matters like the price of corn-plasters and why radio programmes never feature *proper conversations* anymore.

I walked off along the main new-old shopping street. I wondered if the Royal had any excess poundage about her celebrated personage. I hadn't seen her in anything very revealing I thought; a bikini for example, but then she looked quite trim from a distance.

Heading into Mote Street, I spotted here and there the current trend of balding, shaven-headed *older Romeos*. These mature men wore just the right cut of – not too laughably-young jeans, trainers and T-shirts. Just shy of ludicrous, they dressed to discourage women of their own age. At some point they'd dumped their wrinkle-skinned, orange-aiming-for-olive-skinned, bangle-encrusted wives. Like born again twentysomethings they're all *out there* looking for *younger meat*. Equally abundant was the *working man* version, with raffish ear studs in very small ears, set in round feral skulls. Married men, who hadn't gone down the above path of a romantic or sexual *renaissance* let's call it, looked on with a mixture of disdain and envy. They were considering, on the one hand, how wonderful it might be to revisit the sweet breathless bonding and cleaving of youth; knowing again the smell of a young woman, her firm curves, her young and healthy form, realising all the while that she will never come his way again. On the other hand, they were also probably thinking what worthless swine these guys were, abandoning their – probably – faithful partners in later life, after the pain and sacrifice of childbirth, motherhood and wifely duty. But then, I reflected that perhaps this was merely the propaganda of an earlier age. Maybe it referred to a time when men and women leaned on each other more for practical reasons. Perhaps women had previously enjoyed little income of their own, or men feared punishment for the social taboo of leaving a faithful wife. The onlooker hardly dared ask himself. Maybe the final conclusion of this line of thought is simply that this is just how things have always been, and the older man had never realised it until now. Is it, I thought, really that we are only drawn to each other out of a single-minded desire to enjoy the body of the opposite gender? Is it solely about an animal drive to couple, to procreate, bond until the bonding wears off, and the pieces no longer fit together? A moment passes and conventional man is walked-on by his oblivious wife-colleague to new boutiques and cold lunches in front of the TV. These came to him on convenient trays with a cupholder that never allows you to spill your fluids. He watches life and youth and sex and heart-pounding moments dodge backwards like a figure on the platform when the train goes out; distant and all but lost from view. He (and maybe I) sense defeat and settle for the best we can expect; the vicarious pleasures of the kids meeting and matching-up with partners, wedding and producing grandchildren...

This streaming of thoughts was brashly interrupted by the sound of marching music, pomp, drumming and the barking of commands. The band and the crowd I said to myself. I'd best get away from the area before the ritual paralysis sets in and the parade starts. Before the police and their close cousins, the traffic wardens, and police support officers all start up their engines of importance. They'd be out and about soon holding walkie-talkies and sporting shiny badges. Then in their turn came the undercover officers, to a man dressed in an unvarying uniform of brown shoes and tweed jackets, leading lovely velvety-eared spaniels. They may as well have been wearing vests marked *Police undercover*. What a world I thought to myself, what a wonderfully idiot, lop-eared world! Certainly inexplicable events were going on in this atypical town. For the life of me I didn't really get it. What is all this performance for? I remained baffled as the marching and the military barking faded out. I sauntered along towards the castle path. Here, lovers and non-lovers lay about in pools of kindred feeling, mixing private jokes and saliva in the warmth of the sunny day it had unexpectedly and invisibly become. Birds and jets flew high and far off to where the clouds had long since moved along. It was a day of nothing to do until dark. It could, I thought, have been any town in England except for the un-swerveable fact that it was Castletown and the Royal was in residence. I supposed that the Royal would probably understand my sometimes frustrated views better than most, as a personage who had after all seen, met and shaken hands with almost all examples of humanity over in countless odd decades of regalness.

Good egg! I thought. Good egg!

Chunk Three.

Small Arms and Big (K)Nobs

It was the weekend, Saturday to be precise, and rather late in the day, 7 p.m., to be equally precise, I left my cramped but well-placed bedsit to visit more of the good people of Castletown. I thought that the only way to really get to know Castletown, *belt and braces*, was to see folk in their native habitat. I wondered who I would call on first, the Royal? ... Well, realistically ... not ... No, some lowlier members of the human dramatis personae. I resolved to go for a medium hot curry; this usually got the juices flowing! I walked the ten minutes to Castletown Curry House, which was heaving. The good and hungry folk of Castletown loved a curry better than anything else. Inside this particular eatery, I discovered an *Arthurian Round Table* of local characters. I recognised some of the major or pillars (pillocks) of the local community. More specifically, they constituted a group of local council members. I noted: Head of Planning (HP), Mr Trading Standards (TS) and the Council Leader himself (CL). The scene was compelling for its colour and noise. The *Big (K)nobs* sat round and round the *Round Table* as if it was a tribal fire.

"You look like you've lost weight Ted?"

"Yes, I'm on a diet."

"Yes, what diet's that then?"

"It's the *Incessant Nagging Diet*."

"The what?"

"The Incessant Nagging Diet? It's very simple ... my wife nags me incessantly until I stop eating!"

Laughter.

As time passed, the *Pillars* held forth on their chosen subjects. TS was relating a *case* he had been prosecuting against some local *scallywag*. The word scallywag was used to endear him to his peers by sounding laddish. His whole tale-telling was indeed very reasonable in tone. He'd worked hard on the art of saying unreasonable things in a reasonable voice.

"Err ... yes, well, this character had already got the whole scam going when I was, er, called upon shall we say, to ... intervene. It was clear ..."

He looked round the *Round Table* of round-eyed faces to see he was being listened to with the appropriate measure of attention and respect.

"That he ... had, er *no intention* ... (Meaningful looks were exchanged round and round the Round Table) ... of doing the, er, *right thing*, so, I decided to er ... well, shall we say, *'ave 'im!*"

He delighted in using barrow-boy phrases among this crowd of (now merry) *knights-at-arms, his people, his cronies; his town*. It added, he felt, something a little gritty to his delivery and a frisson to his story. He felt like a *redtop journo*, a man who can seek out and destroy rottenness in his local universe. A big (k)nob in a small town!

29

He relaxed into his flow, supplying more detail of his *coupe* against the miserable character.

"Well ..." He went on, "this guy was *actually running*, would you believe?" He paused for maximum effect, "A *gun factory* in his living room! It was like a scene from Butch Cassidy and the effing Sundance Kid!"

At this: guffaws and stifled (rather girlish) noises from the assemblage of Big (K)nobs. Each of the (K)nobs determined at this juncture to make a comment. CL, amid the uproar: "I do hope we are not the United States of America yet!"

While HP chimed in with: "He had all the requisite health and safety paperwork, I hope?"

They dissolved into red-veined mirth over the hot food.

Clicking his fingers at a waiter, "More *Roald* please Mohamed!" CL clipped without looking round. Mohamed was puzzled. CL clarified it a little irritably: "Roald, Roald, you know *dhal – Roald Dhal!*"

He turned and sniggered at the others at the round table and Mohamed also laughed obligingly. He went back to the kitchen and ordered it with a sneer-smile on his face and miming to the others in the kitchen about the old fart upstairs with a large belly who had ordered it. They got to work on more dhal. Upstairs, meanwhile TS was enlarging on his theme about the armchair arsenal in Castletown and was putting together a lurid picture of the culprit.

"This character sees himself as some kind of *war hero* or some-such, an ancient guy, about 95 if I had to hazard a guess. He'd got this *unbelievable* number of replica guns in his front room! I could hardly believe my eyes! There he was, for *all the world*, like some innocent old geezer simply knocking out replica firearms for the hell of it!"

CL decided to chip in here to reinforce who the boss was, in broad terms round the table. "State of play, currently, at this moment in time?"

TS looked round at his audience rather than pay unnecessary attention to CL. He addressed himself more to HP and other *lessers* at the table.

Again, he used his gritty *man of the world* tone. "Well, we *'ad to 'ave 'im*, didn't we?!"

"Took him to the cleaners! Actually, *in the end,* he did turn out to be some little old geezer with a bravery award with a hobby of making replicas, but ignorance is no excuse in front of the law as we all well know! So, he got his comeuppance, silly old bugger!"

He spoke this last sentence as though he was wrapping up a committee meeting. Then, as if pricked by a table-fork, swivelled and snapped with less bonhomie. "Where's that dhal then?"

CL looked over, a little amused by this telltale sign that his-slightly-lesser colleague had not made *such* a great success of his story. He started his own line in entertainment by amusing the *Round-Tablers* with his first case when he was *the new boy* under *Old Trimmer*, a Castle-town council leader in the '70s. All the assembled waited expectantly, only to be interrupted by Mohamed bringing the replacement dhal and wishing them all a very happy meal for the third time, and *would they be liking any more wines, sirs, please?* They all ignored this question, preferring to dive in to the dhal and listen to the boss.

"Well, as you may know, under *Old Trimmer* things were quite different to the council we run today," he started off. "Well, my first case was under him." He continued to *hold court,* until they stood up and made to leave. The bill was settled with a muttered reference to the ten percent gratuity, *not really applicable* and a patronising hand on the arm as the Round Table of *somewhat* equals went to their various cars. It was clear that Castletown had been set to rights over dinner and that full stomachs and self-congratulation reigned over the town just as the Royal did over the castle and the country. What could possibly be nicer I thought as I walked in the trails of their reflected glory back home.

The day had indeed faded away and I was now back where I usually am by nine or ten o'clock in the evening, namely at the absolute, undisputed bull's-eye centre of the universe. You may scoff, but the rationale for this is impeccable. Look, the Royal is head of state in this great land which is, as we all know, the oldest-established continuous democracy in the world (Magna Carta and all that malarkey). So, the Royal is at the centre of everything that is, she is the most significant person anywhere, right? Okay, so said Royal, *our* Royal, is at the heart of the most long-lived civilised seat of power on the planet, *n'est-ce pas?* So, given that the Royal's favourite place and spiritual home is Castletown, Castletown is *logically* the centre of the civilised world, right? Right! Okay, so because the Royal is based here (it's her favourite home), Castletown is *unarguably* the centre of the world. Now, because we don't yet live on any other planet (except for certain people who are mainly under lock and key), Castletown is, as a consequence, **the centre of the known universe**. Now the Castle of Castletown is *nearly* the centre of the universe, but because the Royal only lives here a *percentage* of her time, we can (to be truly balanced) only apportion a percentage or *weighting* for her habitation to the actual castle, let's say forty percent? We must apportion significance and status in a slightly larger percentage to those parts of the Royal's land and estate, which are central to the Royal's presence and substance. We must choose a key position where the Royal is represented in the geographic and sentimental *fulcrum* of the royal spirit and soul. Now looking at the map of (let's call it the *royal presence* in Castletown and environs), in terms of ownership, influence and importance, we end up with a place, by absolute logic, represented geographically, shown to be the centre of the universe. This place as it goes (since I am personally fully prepared to accept the above completely objective analysis), is actually, and out of sheer coincidence, *my armchair in the middle of my bedsit!* In point of fact, and again it's pure chance that it's my chair! I am, I admit, momentarily deranged out of sheer surprise myself, but there it is! You can't argue with facts. My arse, I marvelled, is actually sitting at or on the centre of the universe. Narcissistically deranged as I clearly was, it was still a bloody good feeling! Wow! At the very hub of the universe, is a good place to comment on the world before you, or indeed under you. This world was Castletown and now, a few hours later, I am still viewing the world of Castletown from my top floor bedsit lavatory where I sit imagining I'm dropping large brown bombs on my enemies. At the same time I try to guess what traits of human nature are reflected in/by Castletown. I said to myself, Castletown is really *Everytown*. It's just like Slothtown up the road. Slothtown is just like Castletown but without the (K)nobs on/in. It certainly had slobs in but maybe not as many (K)nobs as Castletown. So a day out in Castletown is a day out in the whole of England. So long as you adjust your sensibilities a little here and there, it's as clear as daylight! Because I was sure of the truth of these thoughts, and that everywhere everyone was actually in the same *soup* (some more primal than others), I realised what had been bothering me for quite a while. It was this: why the *fuck* was life so bloody unfair and so bloody meaningless much of the time? I suddenly felt that I wanted a damn good explanation from someone obscenely self-important as to why this was the case. I wanted, in fact, a summing up from some crumbling high court judge or some stale-wart/stalwart, or community pillar/pillock. Why, I would ask him/her, were having little imagination, not asking questions and towing the line the best credentials for belonging to a town? Belonging to any town, Castletown, Slothtown, Everytown? And why was England, of all great countries, so fucked up? I wanted to know. We may as well replace the ubiquitous and idiotic FCUK with FUKC, FUCKED UP TO KINGDOM COME. Let's all buy the T-shirt! Let's all wear the T-shirt!

I walked for a long while along the river in silent thought. The afternoon was quiet and beautiful and contrasted with my-momentarily-grim thoughts. Sad, bad and dangerous-ly low had we sunk, and there seemed no turning back. The medieval folk who had caroused and fornicated in the streets were still here. They'd merely been *in waiting,* I thought. Here they were, still here, the same people, sim-ply divided by intervals of a few hundred years, but surely the same people, the same faces, the same genes, wearing jeans. Only the names had changed, and even so only the Christian names. Many of the old Castletown families were still well represented. Here they are, sitting outside the all-day alehouses from early morning, swearing, spitting and cackling. They were still here shouting lewd remarks to their womenfolk at the tables, who in turn, were letting out cackles of coarse laughter as though every comment was an invitation to sexual intercourse on the ground, right here and right now. It probably was. I thought that I'd go and see what the folk of this special regal turret-topped toff's town thought of modern life in this ancient setting. Maybe I'd discover what bridged the generations. It wasn't a bridge you could just walk over however, like the bridge from Castletown to Collegetown. I calculated though, that the passage of time was a *blink of an eye*, and the only things to have changed were the stage-sets, the costumes and the shops' names. In a town like Castletown the main stage hasn't really changed at all. The Castle still ruled supreme. I was resolved to find out. I wanted to see things *in the raw*. Truths, I thought, when released still have the power to shock even the experienced observer. I entered an inn and looked around me for information. I didn't have long to wait for evidence that life never really changes. Well, they say there's nothing new under the sun.

"Like a hard time darlin'?"

This from a shapely, young, but experienced-looking blonde at the first table in the bar, with a grin. "I give great head."

I was jolted upright. My outlook on womenfolk had always inclined towards the soft, fragrant, long silken haired pre-Raphaelite type. They would be softly blushing, liquid-eyed goddesses. The perfect confections of my waking dreams had little in common with this, really quite pretty woman, offering me sex served cold on a plate. I looked ahead of me, a little shocked despite a reasonable knowledge of the world, as much as anything from the sheer suddenness of it. This woman, of no more than nineteen or twenty, was standing in a pose of erotic invitation in my face. She wasn't at this point even asking me to part with any money, and I thought that if I'd drunk a few glasses well ... She continued to stand there questioningly. I could have touched her mobile breasts with the tip of my nose from where I was sitting. She asked me again with a more assertive and slightly hostile smile on her lips. "I give *head*," she said again, encouragingly.

"Sorry, I said, I give *mind*" and left.

I did even so, despite the blunt reality of this encounter, want to talk with, or at least *be* with fellow human beings, so I went to a pub called *The Bloated Fascist* in Mote Passage. It may have enjoyed a different name to be wholly honest, but this was the name me and my friends used for it and it was well deserved. It was the lair of a man with a grudge against almost anything that wasn't food or some other gratification for his irascible ego. I have to say he wasn't a clever man or a talented man, but he was *one of us*, and for this reason, in particular, he was unassailable. He was the olde worlde hearth and crackling winter fire of small-town England. Without him, and the likes of him, there would be fewer sanctuaries for other *one of us* locals to go to mildly trash the rest of the world with mildly beery, good humoured bigotry. He was the *insider* and it had to be said, *I* was on the outside in this, his historic watering hole. Regarding the Bloated Fascist, there is much to say, and in it, there was much being said. Men-folk were holding forth noisily on the subject of sport. According to the rule of staying just inside the membrane of acceptability, we can make mildly racist, it's okay, *because he's been adopted as one of us,* asides about the day's sporting winners and losers. Menfolk in the BF were doing this as I entered, in very loud voices full of cocky traditional Sunday *I'm-shagging-this-pert-arsed-blonde-as-soon-as-I get-home*-beer-spittle. Then in comes the BF himself, he who *can* park his four-wheel drive wherever he damned well likes. He can draw up any time in front of his *I own the freehold of this free house of traditional food and serving wenches* pub. *You,* though, can expect the full rigour of the traffic wardens if you have the gall to park near the front of my pub. This is *my* pub mate, *my* town! You may live here, but you're not one of us. *We* all know this, and, by the way, *so too* do the traffic wardens. The BF's *big voice* is everywhere, insinuating that even when he's not there in person, his voice is stored in the brickwork like radiant heat, and resonates back at you out of the ancient six-foot-thick walls. He was *there* like the smell of six hundred years of crackling logs. And of course the other local guardians of the stronghold, the *regulars*, keep the faith and keep the place for him. A *keep* like the BF in a castle-town such as this was always well fortified. To add to this, there is the mote to keep you out, to keep you *remote*. I hummed to myself, *and if you are in you are in, and if you are out you are out ... and if you are only half way in ...* well you know the rest. *I* was definitely *out,* I said to myself. I would never be *in*. I was neither in with the town nor the townsfolk and, certainly, nor was I *in* with the women-folk. They were sticking, stickily close to the fine-tuned, firm-muscled and sharply defined features of the *sports-men*. Men with balls of gold and buttocks of carved stone. These waited casually and indulgently for their evening's moment of completion – of predetermined satis-faction – by rite and well ... quite right! Nothing could be more normal. Certainly nothing was more terrifyingly im-penetrable than these tightly fortressed ranks of local folk. The brigade of woman were of course very penetrable in due course, in the right cause, and were occasionally, very coarse of course! I figured no upstart, *on-the-outside-look-ing-in,* would qualify for such privileges! Anyway, did I really want *privileges* from the women of these physical jerks? I'll give it some thought, I thought.

Chunk Four.

Inappropriate Behaviour

A sense of impending bother was creeping over me in this chilly late afternoon-turning-to-evening, with its stealthily developing shadows. Castletown had a way of thrusting shadows over you like black bats' wings and the castle itself, bristling with medieval mood, produced a particular frisson of excitement-fear as I passed under its sheer grey walls. I was though, cheered by the lights of various bars and hotels that cast warm yellow light onto the narrow cobbled streets. So the feeling of possible bother was soon replaced by a sense of *almost belonging*, belonging at least to the ancient buildings, as I felt I never could to the folk of the town. I sought refuge from the gusty wind in the *Cow and Castle* pub, again named informally by yours truly, because of the green-skinned acid-tempered witch who managed it. When I say she managed it I mean she *reigned* greenly over it spitting acid from one end of its very long bar to the other. She was quite a sight to behold, with arms tightly folded under her chest with a default pissed off expression. She unleashed this default of pissed-off-ness as an unspoken warning to all-comers, but especially at men. She used it especially on men she thought she just might have been married to or divorced from in an un-guarded moment earlier in her life, before she turned acid green and had learned to hate them professionally. She shot out ray-gun beams across her domain, rivalling the Royal for primacy over this castle-facing choicely positioned cheap-and-nasty drinkers' *palace*. The pub owners' were really pleased with her reign of terror, especially her effectiveness in ejecting those among her drinking *subjects* who crossed her. She dealt with these with lightening reactions, and could get a transgressor out onto the street before you could say *serious liver disease*. She was not the AGW for nothing and her kryptonite-like reputation went before her! Anyway I decided to enter her realm on this particular evening since I considered it the best and cheapest way to dispel my boredom. There was a sizable gathering in the drinkers' stronghold, and I wondered why there were quite so many punters around on a Monday night. All became clear when I caught sight of what was meant to be a mirth-inducing poster above the bar, suggesting Monday night was now *Funny Night* at *The Cow and Castle*, in Castletown. That's funny I thought, since I could see absolutely no sign of anybody cracking up. I could hear nothing in the way of the raucous laughter in the measure the poster seemed to promise in large **comic sans**. The poster itself was knee-deep in tickled characters, sporting tears of mirth in their eyes. I felt a little cheated. Then I noticed that the time now was only 7 p.m., thus the mirth-fest was not due to kick off for another hour. I relaxed and decided to have a drink or two, and see if the threats of my sides splitting would live up to expectations. I drank slowly and looked about me at my fellow pre-hysterical gatherers. They were a pretty typical group and I counted off *types*. I was already familiar to most of them and crossed them off on virtual fingers as I observed. My sense of bother was now fully allayed. There was a young fat guy in a circle of other youths alongside an oriental girl, who I figured out after a while, was using his lust as a means of financial support, a bit like social security. There appeared currently to be no obvious benefit to him though, unless of course the continual titillation without any pay-out was enough for him. I thought probably not. She was *dressed to impress* with long silky oriental legs climbing up and up towards, well you know. She flirted mercilessly with him just prior to each round of drinks, then turned away and spoke more intimately to others in the circle once he had waddled all the way up to the bar and waddled back down again with drinks and *snax* from the bar menu. He, for his part, gazed at her continuously and devotedly while she held court to the entire group, with red lips and pouts. He would have gladly put his hand into boiling oil for her. This, curiously, was a deed of gallantry he may soon be in a position to dispatch for her through her uncle, who ran a very prosperous Chinese restaurant in Castletown, and was looking for a kitchen skivvy as luck would have it. The group fizzed and squawked excitedly, migrating in and out of the smoking zone. Out on the smoking terrace of the huge sprawling pub was an off-duty *chef de partie,* having a fag between two tightly pressed fingers and casting sharp glances about at those who may be either friends or bosses from the pub with some reason to question him about something he had done or hadn't done earlier that day/week/month. He looked as though he'd just turned out another batch of food for the deep stainless steel trough that acted as a receptacle for the waiting staff to gouge out fries etc. and slap down onto large plates for the punters *out there*. He eventually finished his roll-up and flicked it dismissively into a dark corner of the terrace setting off in a shifty slightly head-bowed shuffle towards the door. I looked at my watch, still half an hour to go until we were scheduled to be rolling helpless and incapable around the sticky pub floor, so I continued to look around at the patrons. I spotted someone I knew, or at least knew of. The *someone* I knew of was a local character. Actually, he was more a local *caricature*. We know him already as the *Bloated Fascist*. Tonight he was here clearly on a *busman's holiday* drinking away from his own *gastro pub*, as they'd become known. I shuddered inwardly as I viewed his extensive paunch and bearing of supreme pathological self-confidence. He had a clan with him of kindred spirits. I was in a good position to observe him booming out anecdotes.

"Yeah, these bloody little something-year-old kids come in all the time, little *baskets,* just trying it on! I've had to throw them out oh, god knows how many times over the Easter holiday. They get the bloody time off from school to be home studying, but the little buggers just come into my pub to try it on with me! Jesus! Little shits! I don't serve them even when they *do* give me ID. I just tell them to *piss off! Go home and do some work you little shits and don't come back here!* I tell 'em, or *I'll call the law*. That usually works. I don't care what age they are I don't want them anywhere near me."

The assembled kindred spirits laughed long and loud and seemed very happy with their blousey bigoted sense of community. They would have done the same they all sug-

42

gested in word and gesture. They were happily and merrily deep behind their own lines where they could say what they wanted, tightly inside the clan. They threw a wall of defence around themselves; a stronghold; a *keep* of protection. The BF was indeed king of his own castle as he drank on in the *Cow and Castle*, opposite the castle in Castletown.

It was now I first heard noises suggesting the starting up of *Funny Night,* so I turned away from the BF and his entourage to give attention to a couple of zanily dressed men setting up a mic. and other props. I settled down to watch the show proper get started. As if not to be ignored, a trumpeting guffaw issued from the BF, who along with his kinsmen, prepared to move onto another local hostelry the BF could compare unfavourably with his own. He put his stomach outside the door to check the weather, finding it clement enough for the remainder of him to follow, they left. I focused fully on the night of guaranteed comedic entertainment. I was aware as I readied myself, of a group of high-spirited, noisy punters who had *loaded* the pub heavily at the bar edge. They waited expectantly whilst ordering drinks and refills at the same time, so as not to miss a second of the impending hilarity. I drank and watched with them as the two garishly dressed wise-crackers adjusted various items of rib-tickling equipment to get us *in the mood.* To this end, now that they were sort of under way, funny man number one asked a direct question of the crowd. Frankly I considered it to be his first mistake.

"Are ya' feeling funny?" He bellowed.

When the response produced a less than definitive confirmation, he shouted the fateful question again.

"Hey! Castletown (in the style of big-name artistes) are ya' feeling *FUNNY?*"

Well, I had personally to admit that I was feeling a little odd, definitely not funny in the sense that he meant, so I supplied the answer that nobody else seemed inclined to give.

"No, we were waiting for you to *supply* that part!"

Well, I saw this as good old-fashioned heckling, but the AGW (Acid Green Witch) clearly didn't share my view and *whooshed* up the bar like a scene from the *Exorcist* and rang out above the non-laughter.

"Quiet while the artistes are performing!"

I thought about this momentarily and then of course, seeing the inherent fallacy of the proposition, said back, "But it's meant to be Funny Night, surely we can laugh can't we?"

"There's nothing to laugh about!" she shot back sharply.

As the next few minutes elapsed I conceded she was right. The crowd began to get restless fairly quickly, and more than a little sarcastic viz a viz the description given on the notice over the bar. Things were going the wrong way I reckoned in terms of achieving humorous helplessness. Others seemed to share my view and started making comments about the humourlessness on offer. We were all eager to see what would develop. The atmosphere was a touch on the dangerous side, with the comics in the role of prey. They started to get their act together a little and elicited a few ripples of pale laughter from the polite end of the bar. But my comrades-in-heckling-arms were having none of it. They were grouping into a sarcastic semi-circle of beery dissent. The AGW would, of course, have intervened again at this point but she was out back kicking the arse of the *chef de partie* who had unwisely drifted back into the bar. Thus, the sport of killer-heckling continued to escalate for a time. The comics were really quite thick-skinned about it all and continued their act, all the while looking rueful and half-amused at what they saw as a token glitch in any professional performers' route to the top. The crowd, however, was minded to think that they were just *not bloody funny*, and began to say as much. Thus, the heckling itself *became* the performance, and those with a more natural feel for the truly comic started a parallel routine.

"Oi," (to the fatter of the two entertainers) "pork-belly, are you on the stage or on the menu?"

Some real laughter came from this. The funny men looked a trifle rattled at this, but continued.

Another of the semi-circle hecklers chipped in, "Oi, can you get funny now mate? I'm developing FHDS, that's fatal humour deficiency syndrome here!"

The AGW now returned to her realm, doing her impression of a horror movie on fast-forward, whooshing up the bar like something Jack Nicholson would have admired, and leapt into the fray. She directed her venom, I thought a little unfairly, on my buddies and me in the, *you-aren't-bleeding-funny* semi-circle. We bridled at her attack but decided to face the battle with equilibrium.

"What *is* the problem?!" She shouted at me. I was still facing her while it happened that the other traitorous swine had turned their backs. She powered up the bar on the wings of a sulphurous green witch-bat. "Well ...?"

I started off, "What it is, you see ..."

Why I started off like Bertie fucking Wooster in an interchange with Jeeves is anyone's guess, and I certainly had no idea myself. Nerves I guess. If I'd owned a hat I may also have set it at a jaunty angle in order to deal more casually with her dark alchemy and black magic. I was hatless though, so I simply held a gaze that reached into my very soul and said at last, "Well you see, it isn't *funny* is it?"

She looked me up and down and also through me, with green x-ray vision. Her head may have spun through three hundred and sixty degrees a few times at this point too, I suspected.

"You're banned!" she pronounced.

I reeled at this since, as a heckler at probably the quieter end of the heckling assembly, I felt singled out. I spluttered rather it has to be said. She simply turned her back to leave, having made her far-reaching world-shaking decision in the batting of an eye, or rather the batting of her bat wings. I had no chance to reply. I was deeply shocked. I called out, rather loudly, after her retreating satanic figure.

"Why the F.U.C.K ..." I enunciated each letter separately, "am I banned, *may* I ask?"

I said it with some dignity, I can tell you.

She returned as if attached by a rubber band to the spot she had just been in, and shot back at me. "... For inappropriate behaviour and swearing!"

I spluttered further, "Whhhhhhaaaat the f ..."

"*What inappropriate behaviour?*" I demanded to know.

"Not laughing," she said with a snap. Her mouth closed like a steel trap, allowing for no further debate. Then, without turning a hair and without turning round, she was gone. I paused for a second, bereft of speech and breathless with indignation, seeking support and comfort from others of the redoubtable not-bloody-funny-pressure group. But looking at the bar I realised that life around me had moved on. I turned to discover a Polish escort (no not that kind) waiting to see me to the door. I looked around for help but found none. The traitors had either merged with more compliant groups of drinkers who didn't know what funny meant and didn't care, while the hard-core non-amusees had all left. I felt exasperated but temporarily unable to think of a plan. My exit strategy was intended to be loud shouts of *Fascists* and *Comedy-Deniers* but in the end it proved to be two large Poles with steel biceps. What a life I said to myself, what a life!

Chunk Five.

Who Stole the Tarts?

The Queen of Hearts she made some tarts all on a summer's day;
The Knave of Hearts he stole the tarts and took them clean away.
The King of Hearts called for the tarts and beat the Knave full sore
The Knave of Hearts brought back the tarts and vowed he'd steal no more.

What a life! Well I had good reason to ask this question with a due degree of ironic snorting. Castletown was a great gig but I had to keep body and soul together somehow. On the strength of my 2:2 in English and Linguistics from a lesser-known university, I landed a job at a large cake and biscuit manufacturer. I knew I'd never enjoy the job (it wasn't me) but my father encouraged me to take a *sales rep* (short for *reptile* I soon learned) job in order to work my way up etc, etc. I felt it would do for now, being young and in need of funds. It was, too, the kind of work you could put out of your mind at the day's end and do your own thing. I kept doing it and started not to like it immediately, but felt I should make *my mark on it* before I moved onto anything else. To this end, I set about engineering what I hoped would be my *mark*. In fact, I wanted more than this. I was aiming, I told myself, for *a moment of glory*. I wanted a way to get up through the ranks quickly, with a pole vault rather than climbing a greasy pole, I thought. It seemed to make sense. It would be, I concluded, *make or break*. In the end, it produced an outcome I couldn't have guessed at. At the large biscuit stroke cake manufacturer, we were at that time producing a brand new confection (as the company always put it) called *Queen's Fancies*. These were very much like sponge fingers but with jam inside, along donut lines. Not bad when driving round grimy London suburbs all day, caught in traffic. They were light but squashy, crisp but gooey. Not exactly tarts so much as tarts' fingers. Even better, they were free! In fact, I relieved my employer of large quantities from my stock, to take home, finding them just the right thing for an evening in front of the TV. *Free that is* unless you view the depletion of my soul in a job of pure fuck-wittery as payment for eating them. Today, the North-arsehole-Circular was solid and I grabbed at the back seat of my Ford Escort for one of the aforementioned *Queen's Fancies*. It proved, out of the blue, to be a moment of inspiration, and I nearly choked on the *Fancy* as the thought came to me!

"Yes!" I shouted at the top of my voice, and punched the air with my fist. I should explain that this was recently *in vogue,* the trend of punching the air and shouting *yes!* in a very loud voice. It wasn't very English of course, not the habit of cricketers on a sedate green field of play. However, had the Royal herself been there, she too would have done it. I sat in the jam triumphant with jammy fingers. My half-devoured fancy-finger pointed at me; genius it seemed to imply. It pointed straight I felt, past me too, towards Castletown, perhaps directly to the castle itself. In point of fact, I think it pointed directly at the Royal herself. The fancy-finger, it appeared to me, was beckoning to me. Indeed it was doing more than this. Yes, it was *waving.* The finger swayed in front of my eyes like a wand, no more like a sceptre. It said: *Yes you can! Yes you will!* The fancy-finger, as if responding to the auspicious moment *dubbed* me with a spot of thick red jam on my shoulder as it spilled like a drop of royal blood from the sponge-finger end. It was an anointment. This finger had become, in my mind's eye, a complete hand. But it was not just any hand. Here was a royal hand, *the* Royal's hand that we loyal subjects have all grown up with. It was the regal waving hand with its distinctive, unmistakable, airy wave. A wave known across the world to emperors and kings. This wave could now be officially the property of Candid Cakes. It was not just a finger any longer. Our very latest confection had become a *Royal Wave*, not one finger at a time. Not two fingers. It had grown, transmuted, spreading out and taking on new form, new life. Yes, a *Royal Wave*. Five regal fingers of delicious spongy jammy loveliness, brought together as a kind of *royal flush* of finely sculptured, airily waving fingers ... on a ... on, let me think, a *battery operated waving-motion base*! It waved! It *actually* waved, just as the Royal waved. The distinctive motion and the full five fingered hand of airy-crunchy-but-chewy scrumptiousness actually moving in front of your eyes! My God I whispered under my breath. Eureka! Eu-fucking-reka!

My boss didn't like it.

"*You*," he jabbed a stubby non-regal and unsympathetic forefinger in my specific direction. "Candid Cakes, employs *you* ..."

He sneered over-much on the word *you* I felt. "Employs *you*," he continued, "to ... take stock to supermarkets and other designated outlets, and merchandise it onto shelves, Sonny Jim, and *nothing else*! Do you understand the meaning of *nothing else*?" he added.

I conceded that I did, but argued that this was a *big idea* with *huge potential* and one that could *revolutionise the industry* and boost the sales of Candid Cakes. I was all enthusiasm and idealism and ideas and go! Sadly my pug-ugly, stubby-fingered boss was only filled with sarcasm and derision.

"Look matey-boy (I really dislike this expression), either do your job or you *will* be full of *go!* Now get out there and sell some stock! We leave the ideas to the ideas men in the friggin' ideas department, *you* ..." More fat forefinger jabbing, "... you are a sales 'rep' (to you and me sunbeam that means reptile!) and 'reps' do the *shit* jobs until or unless they are not 'reps' any friggin' more. Do I make myself clear?"

Indeed he did.

I went off immediately to start my own production line of *Royal Waves* and to hell with the consequences. This could be the really big pole-vaulting move I was looking for. I was all excited and wanted to get my hands on some dough, ha ha! After thirty-nine and a half attempts I admitted failure. Not failure in my quest, just my own personal failure in my ham-fisted inability to make *Royal Waves*. They just would not stand up! The fingers were already made so this was not really the issue. It was more a matter of bringing them together in a fully functioning regal-looking hand. The fingers needed a firm pastry base and my skills just weren't up to it. The waving mechanism was a further complication I realised, but that would come later. Currently I was stuck on the matter getting my fingers to stand up in a straight but stylish row. They needed to be airy in their appearance and also parted at the correct junctures, not a stiff impersonal *rack* of stiff little fingers. I was looking for more of a Michael Angelo fingers nearly touching-caressing as in the *Creation of Adam* in the Sistine Chapel. The same effect as seen in the intro to the

51

South Bank Show with Melvin Bragg. I wanted a serene, tasteful (and *tasty* of course) image but without the music. It was a gentle but royal hand I wanted, akin to art. At present I was getting Hitler suffering from a rare genetic affliction. I changed tack, by approaching a local baker. He was an elderly but vigorous retired baker actually, thrown onto the scrap-heap, after baking brilliant fresh bread and cakes for decades in the back roads of Castletown. He was finally ousted from his livelihood by third-rate supermarket *smell-factory* bread that haunted the outskirts of Castletown like a good smell. This was my man!

"So, Phil ..." I began, trying to convey to the baker that I was in charge. "What I want is absolute perfection and absolute secrecy, right?"

He looked straight ahead with a default face of half-amused scepticism. His look was one reserved most particularly for young people. This young man (me) who starts telling *you* what life is all about before they've even had their first shag; non-applicable of course as this status was in my case (I can assure you!). I would have told him who was the boss had it been the right moment, which it wasn't. Instead he continued to look at me as though I had arrived on his door-step after a recent drain flushing exercise. Then he looked at the rough sketch I'd put together the night before. He viewed this with an acute floury, short-crusty baker's stare. He looked at it rather too well and for rather too long for my liking. Eventually he sighed and turned a querying-cum-pitying look on me.

"What the *flying fuck* is it?"

I was taken aback. I looked protectively at the frontal elevation of my *Royal Wave*. He noticed this and seemed to understand.

"Well?" he reiterated in the same tone.

"It's a unique new confection concept," I responded weakly.

"Yeah? And what the *flying fuck* is that?"

He clearly liked this phrase and dwelt lovingly on it, unmoved by my youthful enthusiasm.

"Um well ..." I started ... He leapt on this.

"Oh it's an *um well* is it?" he came back at me before I could gather myself.

"Okay, you'd like me to bake you up a batch of *um wells*, right?"

"No ..." I corrected him, "... I was just coming to that. What it actually is, err is ... You see, this is *actually* a *Royal Wave.*"

I explained. "By that, I really mean it's a jammy biscuit with five sponge cake fingers. Now, what I need you to do is *bed it* in a pastry crust at the bottom edge so that the fingers stand up and the hand can be made to actually wave, okay?"

I was pleased I had got this much off my chest, as I was sensitive to his slightly sceptical tone, albeit quite kindly too I told myself.

"Right," he put in, swooping like a large floury taloned bird on my innocent use of *actually* and other waffle I had middle-classly inserted into my explanation. He used my words as a kind of sarcastic battering-ram.

"So, *actually* this is a *Royal Wave,* is it?"

As I say, I noticed a definite hint of sarcasm in this baker's *mixture*.

"And you want me to *bed it* do you?"

I nodded.

"So kindly enlighten me as to what it *actually* consists of and how *actually* are we going to *actually* make the 'effing thing then if you don't mind me *actually* asking?"

He was brutal.

"Are we, I wonder, going to go up to London to see the Queen? Or shall we gate-crash Mr fucking Kipling instead?"

Well I must admit that at this juncture I felt he was not a hundred percent with me on this project and I told him as much. Rather surprisingly he smiled broadly.

"Easy tiger come back in a week and I'll have some done for you, okay?"

I left feeling as if I had been mauled by a large floury baking monster, but left also in a state of some excited anticipation. After all, I reasoned to myself, you don't invent a new cake-mould-breaking confection every day do you?

🏰 🏰 🏰

A week later it was a triumph! Seven days to the hour I was again standing in the small back kitchen with *Floury Phil*. I took up the first ever *Royal Wave* hot off the baking tray as if it was an Oscar and waved it above my head in triumph, hopping around as it burned my fingers. Then, sensing an historic moment in the making, I waved my prized invention in the air as I supposed *she* would wave it, back and forth in that distinctive and regal airy manner.

This was a *Royal Wave, it delights inside and out*, I said to myself. This of course was my slogan too I realised. Later that day I read the blurb I had lovingly put together on my PC, ready I thought for my gob-smacking presentation to Candid's top brass.

New! Candid Cakes *Royal Waves,* "a regal de**light**, simply delicious both inside and out (*out* pronounced ***ayt***!)"

The stress on *light* was a stroke of genius I told myself, conveying the sense of delicacy, so less fattening, and causing the slogan to scan and rhyme nicely too, if you allow for a little posh assonance. I was ecstatic. *This*, I said to myself, *was it*! This was the defining moment of my life and career to date. I would triumph over my peers and visit bitter defeat on other biscuit grandees across the land. This new hand-biscuit fusion was more than either a cake or a biscuit. It was a whole new concept in cake and biscuit history; it stuck two fingers (well five actually) up to other *makers and bakers* and created a benchmark in *haute patisserie*. This was no ordinary confection. It had the mark of royalty upon it. I paused a second in my reverie of self-appreciation.

"Yes!" I shouted and raised my fist in triumph, and not for the first time that month I reflected. I was really *smoking* in my mind and imagination. I also thought what the *Royal Wave* needed was a crest, an insignia. It *had* to be approved with the phrase *as eaten by HRH*. It needed, no it *deserved*, to be dubbed *by royal appointment,* like HP sauce or Lyle's golden syrup, it should be adorned with the royal crest. The lion and unicorn should be stamped delicately onto each one. This was my next job. No, I paused again. No, my next job was the waving mechanism!

This was going to be more of a challenge, I thought, but set straight to work. After two weeks and various costly mistakes later I found myself a guy called *Mechanical* (my name) *Mick* (*I do amazing* things *with little screws*, he told me, *and I don't mean pygmy women*) who said he could do it. I trusted him. Well you have to, don't you? I had given him the plans which again I had amateurishly drawn up. He asserted that he had a *knack with all kinds of tools and stuff*, so I concluded that he was my man. I now knew that design and engineering belonged to those dark arts I would never master. In fact I had worked out that if I had been given every device known to man and all the materials required, had I been stranded on a desert island for fifty years, I would still have managed *not* to have cobbled together what I required to save myself. I would also have been unable to fashion even something as basic as say, a corkscrew. Also, almost certainly, I would have lost several digits from each hand in the process of trying. Natural selection is such a bitch! It was just as well I was protected from myself by all the ingenious developments and inventions of western civilization. Also, I did have faith in Mick, especially as he had given various hopeful signs of understanding what I was looking for and had said that he saw *where I was coming from*, so I was quite happy to let him go ahead. I paid him the £100 advance he said he needed for materials etc. I said I would need the device in a week if this was okay, to which he agreed. I would need then of course, to *marry up* Floury Phil and Mick in sweet but precise baking-engineering union. What a thought!

A week later I had in my possession a device that gripped, or maybe even *embraced* the crust of the *Royal Wave* and swayed it realistically to and fro in a wave that can only be described as stylish, and well, *royal*. It was a breakthrough moment nearly topping the first thrill of seeing my first ever batch of *Waves* hot off the baking tray. It had intrigue and the necessary ingredient of wow! It was a coup, a triumph. Man has an incredible talent I mused, for taking an idea and seeing it through to completion. This seed of a thought was now *a tangible thing* I could touch and feel. It also was something I could use against other green-gilled patissiers of biscuits and cakes. It would send a shudder of envy down some backs and a shiver of delight up others I thought. I was all the time preparing my presentation/ demo, and illustrating a small leaflet to accompany the same on my computer. The *Waves* were to be the cream colour of the sponge fingers and tipped with edible red food dye for nail varnish. I wasn't sure if the Royal wore nail varnish, or if she did, this gaudy shade, but it was the most eye-catching design, and looked good to me. The packs would have the slogan on the front with an image of a delighted upper crust lady (I didn't want to be too specific about *our* Royal obviously, in case I gave offence). So now I had the *Waves,* the design, the slogan and the mechanism all ready to go. Floury Phil and Mechanical Mick had both been working hard for the presentation (I didn't tell them this, of course) and the batch was ready to be showcased in a small batch of twenty *Waves* each in a small box, one for each of the top brass of Candid Cakes, the press etc. I was all ready, setting my sights on, and turning my mind, to the *big day*. Great, except that I then had another brainwave.

"God Save the Queen!"

This exclamation of inward joy was in awe of the final cherry on my waving cake-biscuit brainwave; the final touch, the last and rare ingredient in the cake *mix*.

"God Save the Queen?!" said Mick.

"Yes!" I echoed, "God save the Queen."

"Well ..."

Mick pondered, and then said he supposed that putting the music of God Save the Queen into the *Wave*'s base would probably be easy enough, but added that it would *cost me*. I didn't mind another forty quid, so I paid him and said he would have to work fast since my surprise presentation was tomorrow (though I didn't tell him about it). I accepted that, because of the time constraint only my own *demo-Wave* would enjoy the musical accompaniment. It would serve as an example, but I would have to take especial care of it since it would be the only proper example I had. I also added that if he could put the royal insignia and the *by royal appointment* stamp on too it would be brilliant. He was somewhat *iffy* about this, pointing out that it *wasn't actually by royal appointment was it*? But I countered that *it soon would be*, and *not to worry about it*. It then, I must confess, did run through my mind for the first time as to how my *Royal Wave* presentation was to be worked into the Annual General Meeting of the Candid Cakes

Board and Staff the next day. I wasn't really sure of yet, but obviously when you are working on a daring make or break scheme you don't worry over much about tiny details do you? I went for a walk in the cobbled streets of Castletown, which always seemed to bring inspiration and comfort, and it helped kill time between now and when I would meet up with Mick to take possession of the demo-*Wave* in full sound and vision. I was nervous but excited to see the *all singing, all dancing* and of course *all waving* final example of this history-making cake-biscuit confection fit for a queen!

The streets of Castletown looked quite empty for a Thursday, but I was deep in thought and it went well with my mood of nervous expectation. I went on walking and ended up down by the river, wondering if ducks and swans would approve of my *Royal Waves*. I thought to myself that if they went down well at the presentation I could get Floury Phil to do a few and I would come down here to feed the ducks as I did when I was a kid, only with *Waves* instead of bread. They were bound to enjoy them more than stale bread I reasoned. Also they would be really eager to eat them after seeing the mechanism and hearing the music. There would be a right regal *feeding frenzy* more likely than not. I went through the image of this in my mind. It had to be said that these waterfowl I was watching currently certainly did need cheering up! Jesus did they look down in the mouth! Or at least down in the *bill* I suppose it was. All they were doing was sitting on the water looking really hacked off. I wondered what was depressing them. The moorhens looked positively suicidal. I wondered idly if there was a society I could report this situation to or if waterfowl simply had to snap out of it on their own. God it was a hard life for us all! I was in fact still pondering the matter of how you go about cheering up ducks and other floating depressives when I got to *Mechanical Mick's* place to pick up the final version demo *Wave*. This, I told myself was the last and biggest moment of truth! In biscuit terms it was a *crunch* moment, ha ha!

I was not disappointed. There, in a small elegant clear plastic box was the demo *Royal Wave* that I would use to make my fame and fortune at the Candid Cakes AGM the next day. I took it and gave Mick an extra tenner as a sign of my appreciation. He remarked as I left, "If anyone asks about that *unofficial* official crest mate, I know nothing, right?"

"That's fine," I replied and went home. I didn't get much sleep for the larger part of the night. In the end I over-slept, leaving the following morning just in time to get the late train to West London where Candid Cakes pushed out their numerous sweet smelling products. I was used to a familiar bittersweet feeling over the past couple of years arriving at their gloomy Victorian workhouse style build-ing. It was a mixture of really not looking forward to work, along with a pleasant sweet cake smell wafting out from the large chimneys. It was different today of course. I hurried into my office with my case guarding my surprise presentation from prying eyes. I was getting a clearer idea now of how it would unfold. I knew there would be an *any questions* session towards the end of the general meeting, inviting any however lowly Candid Cakes employee to air any subject, cake related of course, with the firm's top brass. This was to be my moment. I'd *rise to the occasion* like a yeast-laden sweetmeat of the highest calibre. My *coup d'cake* would be the storming of the over comfortable old guard of the cake and biscuit establishment with a brilliant mould-breaking cake creation. I would do it, I told myself, yes I would! I went to *the bog* in the first twenty minutes about six times to adjust my tie/hair/jacket/zip etc and went back to my office just as the meeting was about to start in G2. G2 was a large ex-cake baking facility on the ground floor of the Candid Cakes building, with a smell of stale biscuits about it and a grimy parquet floor. This had been put in when it was decommissioned from baking about fifty years prior. I was used to going across there for *training and development* sessions. I was there now to do something much more significant I thought as I walked to a chair as close to the front as I could manage, and at the very end of a row. This was to be my point of emergence into the limelight and to present my gooey gifts to an unsuspecting world. *This is it* I said under my breath. This would blow the smoothly iced top off the cake-baking world! It was to be the luminous cherry-topped moment of brilliance in my meteorically successful baking-related career.

The meeting was long and tedious and I almost fell asleep at one point from lack of sleep the night before and general boredom. I was awakened in a second though when some plummy voiced cake-Czar suggested that we could have maybe a couple of questions *from the floor*. It was clear from his tone that this was really only a *once-every-so-often concession* to the proles and implied that if you were going to ask a question, be quick about it, and don't rock any unspoken boats or you would, more than likely, be the knave of hearts that gets re-shuffled the next day, or sooner if it could be arranged. These were times well before political correctness had attached itself prosthetically to society. I seized my chance. Getting up hurriedly and quaking with nerves, clutching my briefcase, I ran straight into an idiot trying to sit down in the row in front of mine. I swore at him under my breath, all the more violently so because I had heard a nasty cracking noise inside the case as we collided. It didn't sound healthy, but this was decidedly last minute, and there was nothing I could do about it. Why hadn't I brought a solid attaché case instead of the soft briefcase? Anyway I had shown my hand, and now I had to show my *fingers*!

"I, erm ... have something to say!" I piped up, and walked out to the front of the room where the top brass sat on a dais. Since it was the established convention to ask your question from where you were sitting rather than to leap up and go to the front with it, some people looked at me as if I had probably escaped from somewhere. These looked on their guard, while others wore half-amused smiles as if maybe it was the Christmas Party arriving early. I did my best to steady my nerves and plunged ahead with the presentation anyway. The sickening cracking sound from my briefcase really should have warned me that all was not well. It seemed to me though, that even if one or more of the fingers of the demo *Royal Wave* were damaged, I could always still show them the *movement* of the *Wave* and play the music, and then get another of the undamaged ones to show what a complete one looked like at the end. To add to this, I could always make them laugh with a witty comment about the clumsy idiot who damaged the one example I was using. All would have been well ...

"So ..."

My manager put a spin of heavy sarcasm into his question. "... This is *your* brainwave is it, this obscene *biscuit-hand thing? You're* the genius behind the mangled digits on this ... this deformed *stump* with Candid Cakes all over it? It's all *your work*, right down to the tinny God Save the Queen while sticking its middle finger up at the top brass?"

My manager had no sympathy and no soul. I muttered something vaguely defensive under my breath.

"Sorry, *what was that*?"

He glared at me, putting a sarcastic cupped hand to a large florid ear. "Sorry?" he continued, "Did I hear it wrong? Was it *not* a rendition of that tune we use to honour our gracious majesty, but used as a limp and malformed *up yours* gesture with simulated blood every where? Was that *not* what we all witnessed transfixed with horror, in hushed silence while the top brass of Candid Cakes looked on in frozen disbelief? Or maybe it was all a horrible dream?"

"Well, it was jam not blood," I reasoned.

"Oh, oh!" He rejoined in an unusually squeaky voice, "... Oh joy, it was jam was it? *So sorry*, well that's all okay then, so long as it wasn't what it looked like, because what it looked like was that you had cut off four of the royal *fucking* fingers and she was, consequently bleeding to fucking death and telling everyone to *eff off* while she was doing it! That's what it *looked* like to me, but maybe I'm just being too sensitive, right?"

I must admit I quite admired the feeling he put into this speech and actually his quite creative use of language. He was though, attacking me, so I looked less than appreciative. He had clearly left his *bon homie* on the bus or whatever means he used to get to work, so we simply paused and observed a silence for a minute or so. He broke it at last with a resigned noise in the throat that sounded almost kindly.

"Well, *young fellow-me-lad*, we will be sorry to lose you *in a way,* but *top brass* were not amused by yesterday's royal mutilation episode, and the worst of it is that they had a 'journo' in the room from the local *rag*. He was *meant* to be doing a story on the increased profits of the business and Candid Cakes job creation plans, but well, your grotesque effigy of someone giving an unusual royal hand gesture sort of *captured his imagination* a little more. He happened to have his camera at the ready, as you can imagine, being a *hack*, and this will surely be all over the front pages of the local paper on Friday, and it may not stop there. This could go national or god forbid, sunbeam, global."

I must admit that this last comment cheered me up a touch and suggested that all may not be lost. After all there's no such thing as bad publicity I suggested. He disagreed forcibly on this point, gave me my P45 and said that he *wished me luck*. He also remarked that maybe the world of cakes was not really *my thing,* and that perhaps I should look around for something into which I could pour my *creative side*. I thanked him and said that I would clear my desk. He answered that this had already been *done for me* to *save me the trouble*, a cardboard box was *at reception*, and that I would receive my *severance* in the post. He winced at the word severance I noticed, and I reflected that it may have brought back images of the royal fingers, so I didn't linger. I simply replied with a final *thanks* and left Candid Cakes for the last time.

Chunk Six.

Beyond all Doubt Unreasonable

I didn't know it yet, but my major troubles hadn't really begun. They weren't long in coming though. Three days later I had a letter from Castletown Trading Standards asking me in for a meeting, to be conducted *under caution*! I quaked slightly at first but convinced myself quite quickly that there was no *real problem*, after all it was only an internal company presentation and it had been all over in the twinkling of an eye. The top brass hadn't been amused, but then they clearly had no sense of humour, and were generally sour, pompous arses. I was slightly puzzled though about how the matter had come to the attention of the Castletown authorities, and so quickly. Somebody, I conjectured, must have *snitched*. They were a special bunch, Castletown Trading Standards, and when it came to dealing with knaves and scoundrels on their own doorstep they invoked all the special powers derived from –

almost – *royal prerogative*. Having much more disposable income at the ready than scummier, dirtier towns elsewhere in the land, they could really get you by the *short and curlies* if they had a mind to. As it went, I found out they didn't have a mind between them, but they *did* have both strong will and a developed sense of vengeance. Also, I discovered, they had lashings of good old-fashioned prejudice to help them in their job. They were certainly not going to allow anything to besmirch the name of Castletown, and I suspected, would go pretty ballistic if it came to sullying the name of the Royal too. This was the thing that somewhat nagged at me as the date of the meeting came closer. I studied the letter they had initially sent for signs of impending bloodletting and torture. Was this a *tower* job, I wondered? After all, it had brought the sovereign into a light that she may not find funny. She may not be amused. It was, though I considered, much funnier than *Funny Night* at the *Cow and Castle*, but this was not saying much!

The letter read:

Dear Mr ...

It has come to our attention that you may have been making unauthorized use of the royal crest and other related matters. We would like to discuss this with you <u>as a matter of urgency</u> (underlined). We will need to conduct an interview with you "under caution" and would ask you to come prepared to give full details, with supporting paperwork where appropriate, to help respond to our questions. The date of this meeting is scheduled for April 13th, which is a Friday, at 2.30 p.m. at our offices (see above for the address). Please let us know if there will be any difficulty on your side in keeping this appointment, with reasons specifying why, if this should be the case.

Yours etc

Castletown Trading Standards

I noted that they did not sound especially sentimental, but beyond this it did not, either, give a great deal away. I decided to wait until the meeting took place and not give it any more thought. I would be direct with them; I would take my illustrations, my leaflet *and* some *Royal Waves*. This would put them in a good mood; maybe I would get a commission from it; something to do with Castletown Castle? Perhaps it could end up with working for the Royal herself. There was, I thought, possibly something good to come out of this after all. I mean, how upset could they possibly be? I was simply a loyal subject offering the royal personage a bit of free publicity. In a place like Castletown, this was virtually a civic duty I told myself ... I was young at the time, you understand?

This was not though, to my mouth dropping surprise, how they saw it. They were also not really very sentimental *in the flesh* either. They were, once I had been in their company for some five or six seconds, a little bit bad-tempered I reckoned. It had been a pleasant walk up to the ugly new building in Mote Street, which stood out like a very pink national health sticking plaster against the sober elephant grey of Castletown Castle's steep-walled vastness. First the *poetry*, now the *prose* I thought.

"This is a tape machine ..." the first inquisitor proclaimed with a look of proprietary affection. He stroked the machine as you might a large savage dog before offering up its first square meal in a very long time.

"... And this..." he motioned to an unnaturally still, young-ish woman in a black baggy, slightly hippy-style dress, "... is my colleague."

His colleague betrayed no discernable signs of personality, and *helloed* in a detached and vacant voice that may have been intended for a small spider in one corner of the windowless room in which we all were. There *was* a small spider there I had noticed when I first came in, and I felt she was possibly related to it in spirit at least, since the greeting was not intended for anyone else that I could detect. I concluded it *was* indeed for the spider and listened further to the inquisitor I had dubbed *Number One*. He was a more animated soul, *Number One*; moving about the small cell-like room as though he was on the stage in an absurdist drama from the 1950s and knew his part off by heart. I was really, I felt like, an on-looker at a performance, and could only conjecture where and when I was to play my own part. I looked at my bag gaping slightly, with the few *Waves* that I had toyed with offering to my hosts, but began to feel they really didn't deserve them after all, and that my original plan of cheering up the depressive Castletown waterfowl was a better one. *Number One* went on.

"We require you to answer some questions about the matter of protected images, insignias, crests and such like. Is this something you can help us with? Please answer *yes or no*, for the machine."

He directed a tender look towards the *Machine*, much as a doting father might on a favourite son. He then turned a less benign inquisitorial raised eyebrow on me. I felt a little rattled at this point but thought that things were bound to *look up* when I came to my watertight explanation of the facts. I had what you might call a Macawberesque view on this spot of bother and was really expecting something to *turn up*. It did. It was though, not the kind of *turning up* I was hoping for. From a cupboard which had escaped my notice until this moment, *Number One* produced, as if part of a slick conjuring routine that I reckoned he practised far into the night, a plate on which sat my prototype – lovingly created – musical, two-fingered crumpled *Royal Wave*. I started a little I can tell you, looking down at my own case and trying to decide if *Number One* or possibly even *Spidery Woman* had somehow drugged me, stolen my confections and fiendishly reawakened me after putting everything back as it was, in order to send me mad or something. I started again as *Spidery Woman* got up without any obvious ulterior motive and came very close to me indeed and looked at me intently before bringing the *Wave* within a millimetre of my nostrils. She had taken on, I decided, a sinister turn to her persona, even stiller, blacker and more spidery. She addressed her confidante sitting in the very corner of the ceiling and, no doubt, talking in her carefully spun words like a food supplement. I was really very put out.

"You ..." she argued, seemingly to me, but of course she was really talking to her spider-sister on the ceiling, "... you have been identified as the probable person behind the production of these biscuits or perhaps, cakes. Do you accept that you are the said person?"

The spider glared down at me tiny-ly from its safe corner of the cell-room. I knew it would be nodding its small woolly black head accusingly.

Number One, not to be upstaged chipped in. "To the machine please, to the machine!"

He looked over apologetically at *the Machine* as if to say, *there, there my lovely, soon, soon you shall be fed. Spidery Woman* started to circle me like a very large hungry-looking, silent, spider, spinning no doubt an invisible sticky encircling web to imprison me and suck my blood. She would feed me, of course, to her devilish small relation; that is whatever was left of me the machine hadn't first consumed. It would take them a few years I thought to get through the whole of me. Then again, maybe there was a whole colony of small machine babies and spiderlings in another room. The web was closing in around me I thought, and I didn't like it, not at all. I decided to ask a question to break the spell and hopefully call off *Number One*, *Spidery Woman* and her fiendish arachnid sidekick.

"Will there be an opportunity for me to tell you what happened?"

I directed this at *Number One*. I felt at least that he appeared to be securely on my side of the species barrier. He looked at me impatiently and returned.

"Well, this is the *very start* of this process; you will have *ample opportunity* later on to *put your case*." I immediately crossed him off my *possibly human beings* list and looked bleakly ahead of me. The room seemed to get smaller as I sat there, and I was beginning to think that I would probably never get out alive or at all, even dead. I wondered if the room had a secret passage where *Number One* and the spider *odd couple* concealed and devoured members of the surplus population. Instead of an early end to my life though, *Number One* suddenly put his large face up against mine and said in a completely different tone.

"Cup of tea?"

I started jumpily again as though possibly tea was the means of my dispatch. This I conjectured may be an *Alice*-type demonic tea party with me playing the dormouse.

"Yes please."

My reply however was mainly just to see if the door still worked and normal life continued out in the corridor. I got a reassuring glimpse of normality as *Number One* put his head out into the real world and intoned, "Tea in four for three please."

He then moved closer to the *Machine* and said in a loving whisper into what would have been its ear ... "I have offered (my name) refreshments."

This I thought, was rather a *large* word for a cup of tea, but said nothing, not wanting to rock the boat of undead council workers. I waited quietly for another question. *Spidery Woman* got up again. I remember thinking I wish she wouldn't keep doing this, since she seemed to rise out of her chair silently, like smoke, without prior warning and drift noiselessly across the room, no doubt with malign intent. She got up actually only to answer the door to the tea, no biscuits. How she knew the tea was being brought in at that exact moment I have no idea because I for one didn't hear any knock. I put it down to another of her dark arts and listened to *Number One,* who was again in questioning mode.

"What we are asking is, did you in fact *concoct* this," he gestured to the mangled *Wave,* "transgression against trademark law?"

I bridled slightly at this, wanting to get the name straight with him. These were *Royal Waves,* not *transgressions.*

"What the machine needs to hear, for the ... eer record if you like, is did you cause these ... eer cake-biscuit products to be ... eer created and also cause them to bear the legend: *By Appointment to her Royal Majesty* etc.?"

I started my answer.

"Well I suppose ..." only to be cut off again with...

"Either *yes* or *no* for the benefit of the machine please."

The word *yes-ish* came to mind and I would have used it but guessed it was not in the machine's bank of accurate words. I delayed a moment only for *Number One* to repeat the question he had asked a moment before, word for word.

"Either *yes* or *no* for the benefit of the machine please."

"Yes but ..." I started off, but *Spidery Woman* had already written it down and the *Machine* made a sort of decisive clicking noise as though it had passed judgement on its own account. It suggested finality in its click, and that it wasn't accepting any further information. *Number One* had even moved seamlessly onto another question. I made a *humph* noise and cursed the *Machine* to myself as another tool of evil.

Number One asked, "Do you know that the royal crest is actually protected by a number of laws?" And then quickly, in order to cut off any answer which was in the grey zone added, "Again, yes or no, will suffice."

I felt, I must say, that *yes* or *no* would certainly not suffice. I was sure that *yes* or *no* was simply a way of saying *we'll 'ave you with our incriminating yes or no option in the end mate, because that's the system. It's our cunning yes or no board game where you always land on the square marked guilty.*

"No, I didn't know that," I answered.

He accepted the extra wordage with good grace this time and smiled to the *Machine* as though he had passed on a nice little appetizer. There will be more later my lovely though he seemed to imply in his manner. The *Machine clicked* again as if it was swallowing. It was all very unnerving. *Spidery Woman* had decided to rise up soundlessly again; it was a jolt. She went over to the corner of the room and I felt almost certain she would summon her tiny colleague in the far corner of the ceiling to join the meeting. Instead she simply turned round and sat down again. Some form of mind game I thought to myself.

"It is contrary to sub-clause twenty-seven, part thirty-six of the Something, Something Act of some year to reproduce, manufacture or replicate, the Royal Insignia and or to cause it to be represented or portrayed on any product or in any form which may be considered a misuse of its intended purpose," she quoted half to me half to the *Machine*. "Do you understand this point?"

Then added, as if benefiting from the wisdom of *Number One*, "*that requires just yes or no please.*"

She didn't add, *to the machine* here, I suspected, because she wasn't as intimate with it as *Number One*.

"No, I didn't," I reasoned hopefully.

"Well, given this fact, we will be interviewing you, and possibly others, regarding possible offences under the said Act and what, if any, charges we may be bringing regarding the same."

I felt I was in the centre of a multiple-choice nightmare with any number of possible outcomes, all of them unpleasant. I wasn't sure I was called upon to reply at this point, and was just about to when *Number One* did his *A* or *B* option game again, again to be clicked at by the *Machine*. The mood of the meeting changed a little from this point, in that *Number One* had decided it was that time of the day for *show and tell*. He gathered up the sorry looking *Royal Wave* and examined it in the style of an expert on the *Antiques Road Show*. If he'd had an eyeglass he would certainly have used it. He murmured softly to himself as he studied the royal crest, coming over to me with his finger on the offending lettering. To the *Machine* he noted: "I am showing (my name) the insignia on this sweetmeat product." To me he said, "Do you recognize this mark?"

I said that I did. He continued: "Did you stamp, or did you cause these letters to be stamped on this sweetmeat may I ask?"

Again, my choices were limited, and I wondered if anyone ever got to elaborate about their motivation; the thrill of having an idea; the excitement of inventing something and seeing it through from germ stage to completion. Did these creatures not understand the significance of breathing life into a seed of virgin thought I questioned myself?

He was obviously reading my thoughts through some dastardly mind-warping method that was, for now, unclear.

"What we want to ascertain, (my name) *only* is whether or not you have broken a law or laws relating to the Act or Acts that we have mentioned to you. Do you understand my meaning?"

I put him a couple of notches even lower still in the *Chain of Being* and responded with the answer we had been practising all afternoon, "Yes, but ..."

He moved on and so did the *Machine* with its twisted clicking, one-track mind. When I emerged into normality and daylight in one piece, I was pretty surprised and relieved in equal measure. I hadn't *got over it* though. I was certain I'd be visited, if not literally, at the very least in nightmares by *Spidery Woman* and her tiny sidekick. I reckoned they'd wish to glue me to the recently vacated interview chair, like a juicy human fly. *Number One* would be there too, frantically banging on my door, carrying the *Machine* lovingly under one arm, making its sharp clicking noises like the gnashing teeth of a small square madman.

Chunk Seven.

Cogs and Wheels

My next port of call was the *law-monger, which* was conveniently situated above the fishmonger, making the law and food that looked like lawyers, very much a *one-stop-*

shop. I was quite pleased about this as I fancied a bit of smoked haddock anyway, being Friday. I rang the bell with my haddock in hand and was finally, after a number of *coming towards the door* noises, let in by an ancient English gentlewoman with sensible brown shoes and a huge bosom. She suggested imperiously that I wait in the room marked *Waiting and Copying.* In the room was a genuine antique photocopier about the size of a small rhinoceros and about as sharp I reckoned, looking at the vast extrusions of 1970's plastic cowling, rivets and screws. The huge-chested woman came in as I squeezed with difficulty between the copier and a hideous 1930's sideboard arranged with dry-looking magazines, asking if I would like *tea or coffee.* I deliberated and chose tea. Coffee, as I think we have already learned, is not reliable in England, and I had decided many years ago not to risk it, since it is composed of equal parts cleaning fluid and soap. Tea was a more natural choice and couldn't be sabotaged without great determination. I settled down to the statutory wait with the mug and looked at the lawyer's *Waiting and Copying* facility in more detail. It had all the standard features of a small-town *law-monger.* In one corner was a dead pot plant, which having expired (I'm no expert you understand, but clearly more than a year before) was shrivelled but dignified in death, standing straight, brown and leafless like a small mummified tree from a long-dead civilization. Along the walls were standard issue volumes of the *Law Society Gazette* or some such racy periodical, Issues 0-500 sporting the odd change in design and binding along the way, every hundred years or so. I looked closer to see if I could catch out any interruption in the perfect symmetry and sequence of the volume numbers. No, they faithfully charted legal milestones down the years. Clearly they were being *kept up* by an obsessive-compulsive who had seen people like me coming and set out to thwart us. Also, almost present in the room was a carpet, which had been of good quality when carpets were first invented. The craft had moved on though, and this fine example had moved on too, thread by thread on clients' shoes. It was now a series of strings attached by some brown tape, in a loose web-like pattern on a background motif of floorboards. The word *web* made me shiver, suddenly bringing back visions of *Number One, Spidery Woman,* et al. I looked over at some of the yellowing legal posters still hanging stubbornly to the walls.

One said: **Are you represented?** Another asked: **What Price Ignorance?**

They didn't actually give a figure I noticed. I spent some time speculating on the price of ignorance therefore wondering if it came in bags of a pound or kilo, or simply loose. I was disturbed finally by the massive chested woman.

"Ms Updyke will see you now."

Why, I thought, as I snaked my way up the stairs to a smelly back room, why, since I was neurotically punctual, did I *never ever* get to see any legal personage except after at least a fifteen-minute wait? I had never turned up to be presented fresh-faced and eager in front of a bright smiley lawyer at the time arranged. Today was no exception. I was shooed ahead of the advancing bosom into the presence of Ms Updyke, well named I thought to myself as I was introduced. That she wasn't a Miss or Mrs became very clear from her aging, scrubbed and boyish bearing. In fact she would have been better named Mzzzzzzzz Updyke, with sound effects supplied by a bumblebee the size of a small hovering sheep.

"Sit down please," she suggested without looking up.

"I've been looking through the papers you sent across. Now, potentially we have here, a serious situation. This could be a matter of getting you out of a very tricky predicament, if indeed we can. So tell me, from the top, what happened?"

She inclined a face closer towards me that made me jump back a little, which I hoped she didn't notice. She was, as mentioned, a highly scrubbed looking woman of between thirty and eighty (being precise was difficult because of the nature of her scrubbed skin which had probably been sanded-down by an apprentice painter). I reckoned from her voice though that she was nearer thirty than eighty. She looked at me inquiringly and said, again, encouragingly: "Just the facts please."

She stopped me after a few minutes of my *getting things off my chest*. I felt much better I must say, since I had been pretty spooked by the *Addams Family* at the council offices the previous week and needed solace. I wanted to shine out as an upstanding citizen, a pillar of the community that I truly was. Finally though, she put up a sandpapery hand to allow her to cut in.

"I think," she said with decision, "we should start again with me asking a few questions in order to well, get to the facts of the matter. Now, once you had put together, without your employer's knowledge or permission, a series of these prototype cake-biscuit products, implicating several third parties in the process, you interrupted a scheduled meeting at your workplace to expose them to your invention with both their name on it and bearing the royal crest also used without permission, and caused, as I understand it, a bit of a scene? Is this what happened?"

I felt that she had really misunderstood her role here as my friend, ally, confidante and payee. I was miffed.

"Well," I started off.

"It was all to do with this big idea."

"Yes."

She queried rather sharply I thought, "What was *the big idea*?"

She sounded less sympathetic than I had been banking on, and I didn't like her tone on the matter of my invention, or its sticky end. She would expect payment for this too I thought with irony. She was still looking sandpaperily expectant, so I continued with dignity.

"I felt at the time, and still feel in fact, that my invention and my plan to bring a new and exciting product to the attention of a grateful public has been rather misunderstood."

I eyed her warily during this *pitch* since she hadn't looked especially convinced or impressed. "Well."

She started, again in an unpromising tone, "I doubt *that* will convince anyone at all, quite frankly. As a grown man I should have thought you would have a more realistic view of things too. If you go to court with this, the judge and jury are just going to be irritated. *Going round the houses* with excuses is the worst thing you can do."

"Oh," I was confused. "What should I say then?"

She shot back quickly, "They simply want to know if you did what it is suggested you did or not, nothing else. They don't want to hear *why* you did it or *what* you hoped to achieve by it. Jurors are busy people fulfilling a civic duty. They don't want to hear about your life or your *so called* invention. They will be ordinary members of the public with not much patience."

"Meaning?" I queried.

"Meaning they will be tired, hungry and worried about the things they would normally be doing before they were interrupted to *try* you. They will *not* be amused if you start dodging or avoiding questions or giving opinions. They will, I suggest, get very irritated very quickly."

I concluded at this juncture that things had taken a turn for the worse. This sandpaper faced law-monger was worse, if anything, than my visit to the civic crypt of the other day. What is more, she was painting a picture of a system that threw the book at you as soon as you showed up and tried to answer questions. The famed balance and fairness of English legal processes seemed to consist, in reality, of a smooth conveyer belt of villains efficiently questioned on the *yes* or *no* system so beloved of *Number One*, and then all nicely *banged up* before teatime, all *done and dusted*. As a young well-educated boy from a *nice* family it was truly a rude awakening. I'd been imagining a scene more on the lines of the theatrically distinguished barrister. In my mind he was a Perry Mason, thumbs in waistcoat, his sharp legal brain extolling the merits of a *young man* with *considerable promise,* simply exhibiting a *flair for inventing things.*

Ms Updyke brought me out of this reverie by saying in a vigorous *work-woman-like* manner, "So what are we going to do about it, is the question?"

It *was* indeed the question, and I had an impression something was required of me at this point but I couldn't for the life of me think what it was. I looked at her for a clue. She tut tutted.

"What we need is a defence or at least something that will help *in mitigation*," she went on.

"We need a damned good explanation for your actions and then we can see if we can get a less harsh outcome for you. At present you are a bit of a hopeless case."

She really was a nasty shade of scrubbed pink. This was coupled (I had become aware) with a developing smell of raw fish. For the first time I felt that the fishmonger should have *followed* this legal escapade. I fidgeted in my chair and fiddled with pockets and papers.

"What I wanted to achieve," I recovered, "was a *first* in cake/biscuit fusion. The *Royal Wave* that we have here..."

I whipped one out of my jacket, "brings together all the majesty of HRH's regal and famous wave in a delicious cake/biscuit experience. Now I know that not everyone will be sympathetic towards this but what I was trying to do was quite innocent."

Ms Updyke cut in again here with a simple solution to my idealistic view. "Nobody will be in the least interested in that. You have used a symbol of the Royal House and indicated that this product of yours is connected *with it*; that *she* supports and *uses* the product. This is clearly not the case is it?"

She was beginning to sound as though she had been taking lessons from *Number One*, and I was almost certain she made a final clicking sound in her throat reminiscent of the *Machine*. It was disconcerting. I had expected at least a sympathetic hearing from someone who I probably intended to pay for her services. In place of which I was on the rough end of her sandpapery façade and gritty truth about a hard cold world.

"What I think we should do," she added, "is for you to start at the beginning while I write it all up on the computer. This way we will have a formal defence when it all comes to court if this is the route the Castletown Trading Standards takes."

This was another nasty jolt. It was becoming dangerously like an *open and shut case* with the operative words focusing on the opening of a cell door and then the shutting of it, with me on the wrong side. Not good.

"Can you smell something odd in here by the way?" she put in, tilting her abrasive head to one side like a small sandpapery looking bird. I feigned not smelling anything and tried to divert her from the subject.

"I want simply," I pointed out, "to be judged on the basis of my intentions. I wasn't *trying* to deceive anyone, really. I simply wanted to come up with a unique product that would raise the profile of Candid Cakes. *All this was for them*, in reality."

She looked sceptical. "They will think that a bit fishy."

This dramatic irony was magnified by a waft of haddock spiraling out of the damp packaging in my carrier and snaking its way cartoon-like towards her serrated nostrils.

"I think it best if we," she looked at her watch, "reconvene on another day for the dictation of your Official Statement. Please see my secretary on the way out to set a date. Also I think that you need to take time to get your story straight to counter the Council's case. They are very vigorous about this sort of matter here in Castletown. It would have been better if this had come up somewhere else."

She looked rather pointedly at my bag and said again as if to hurry me along, "That's all for now, thank you."

I left feeling at a low ebb. It seemed to me that the massed forces of Castletown officialdom had got together at a satanic ritual (probably in local woodland) which only certain people know about, like the Freemasons only worse, and had signed up to a blood-pact to *get me*. I couldn't really see what harm had been done myself, after all nobody had been injured, no one got hurt!

The article read:

Gilt comes off the Gingerbread at Candid Cakes!

My god! I thought, people read so much into the smallest things. It was only a little presentation after all, a few pompous old farts put out, why so much fuss? I read on. *Candid Cakes,* the West London based cake-biscuit manufacturer, had been on course for a very profitable year with a number of flagship new products in the "*piping* bag". Then, at an AGM of the firm's top brass, employees and others, a bizarre stunt by a deranged employee turned the sweetmeat producer's board sour. The man, who cannot be named at present, had worked for Candid as a sales *Rep.* He has now been relieved of his duties, but not soon enough to stop him exposing the firm to ridicule in front of top bosses. Members of the Board witnessed him wielding (*wielding!* – this was outrageous, no *wielding* took place I muttered) an obscene and deformed image of *the royal hand* giving an insulting gesture of a kind more at home at a football ground. It added later in the column, this paper has not been able to get any comments from the royal household, but almost certainly they will not be amused! The paper then suggested the reader turn to *financial news*, on page five, to read an article entitled *Sour Dough*, on how this incident may affect Candid's profits!

This was I had to concede, seemingly unstoppable. I thought back three weeks. I was on the *crest of a Wave* so to speak, with my invention set to take an unsuspecting world by storm. Now the storm was breaking immediately over me, threatening to blow me like a loose cigarette paper directly into choky for the rest of the foreseeable. I went out. What inspiration could I get from a walk round the medieval fortress town of Castletown I wondered? I needed to get a clear head for the problems I was up against. I eventually wandered into the *Continental Market*. It wasn't a real English market, but one stage-managed periodically, to push French, Italian and Spanish farm and other natural produce over the English Channel every first Saturday in the month. A small tsunami of unpasteurized dairy goods and flotsam of pastries came over, which outdid the efforts of the local Asian shop's *Jammy Dodgers* made in East Acton, hands down. They closed off the roads to traffic to confuse the locals and made us all feel as though normal life was in suspended animation. The spell was only broken at 4 p.m. when the stalls closed down and slowly evaporated, leaving shreds of French flag, olive stones, and drips of icing sugar where donuts had once been. I arrived just at this anticlimactic moment and also as the rain had just set in professionally, as only English rain knows how. I didn't have an umbrella and was about to dodge into the Tower Café to avoid a soaking. I nearly did go in but thought better of it, concluding that it wasn't the day for this. Instead I went back to my digs, again keeping myself to myself. I thought *better in than out* tonight. This Saturday, I said to myself, would be a wild and windy night in Castletown.

I did, though, go back to the Tower Café at about the same time in the late afternoon after work, on the Tuesday following. It was raining again. I went back so soon in need of reconnection with my train of thought from the Saturday. The café, I soon realised, was a *stickler* for old-fashioned teas; there was not a croissant to be seen. I scanned the *Tower Menu*, which had been cunningly fashioned into a cut out of a castle's turrets. It had been conceived in medieval metaphors, especially with reference to castles and connected notions. I looked at *savouries*. Under this heading were *soft-boiled eggs and soldiers in bearskins,* the explanation being toast *soldiers* with Marmite at one end, thus bearskins. Then you could also choose a *Castle Burger*, which consisted of a *parapet* of a 100% beef burger, *reinforced* with optional cheese, plus a surrounding *mote* of either French fries or salad, described on the menu as *a substantial feast for an invading army of hungry warriors*. The *sweets* also paid homage to Castletown's history, citing a *Turret-Torte*, described as b*attlements of chocolate torte with a portcullis of white chocolate,* all *on a field of strawberry sauce.* I decided I wasn't in this for a full meal, settling on the *drawbridge biscuit*, a standard shortbread biscuit only glamorised by *the name, and a* *strong cup of Tower Café Tea.* I reflected that *Royal Waves* would have given the place much more cache. The tea came in the standard scalding metal teapot, with a complementary leak-as-you-pour function. This refreshment saw me through the shower and gave me time to ponder what was next on my list of possible ways to appease Castletown's outraged civic guardians. I sought some inspiration as I looked across the grimy rain streaked road at the Castletown Tourist Office. It looked fairly empty at this point in the day except for a few *last minute tourists* seeking rooms, who having left booking rather late in the day, were willing possibly, to trade in their 11 a.m. demands of: *we will only accept en-suite room* or *we will really have to go back to London tonight if you are sure that's all you've got,* for humbler constructions such as: *yes we will take that so long as it's clean,* or *well it's only for one night honey.* And so the evening came gently over Castletown. The honest and irritating folk of the town were making their way home or *meeting up* with others coming off early evening trains from London. They were togged up smartly rather than tartily, being a Tuesday, looking forward to an early weekday meal with *the girls from work,* and definitely not, on such a day, willingly to be preyed on by the opposite gender. That would be for Friday and Saturday nights when they would go out in all weathers wearing a small band of elasticised cloth over the upper and lower *significant zones* of the female form. This, a weekday night, and the attentions of men were subject to an unspoken ban. Instead tables of cash-rich office workers, still living at home with their parent or parents, were out to meet *Rachel and Zoe* at the Castletown Wine Bar. That was where they would meet after a blow-by-blow mobile conversation recounting each step of the way each was taking from three separate points. Minute by minute, they checked, both together and separately, to confirm what stage of the journey they were at, *en route* to the meeting place. Squeals of laughter issued down the lines as they beseeched *Wendy* who had already *got there* to order a bottle of Pinot Grigio in time for when they arrived. The *already theres* meanwhile sat about in small incomplete groups waiting for that moment when they could scream and rush over to any new arrivals, greeting them with continental-style kisses on both cheeks. The moment they sat down, shiny mobiles called them away to other squealers with assorted tinklings and buzzings. I could hear nothing from where I was sitting in the Tower Café, but was quite familiar enough with my modern-medieval man and woman to guess. Nothing much had changed over the past several hundred years I mused.

This aimless musing was taking me no further however towards a solution. Not for the first time I pushed myself to determine a course of action. I would see Ms Updyke again but this time I would have my story as watertight as possible. I went back to my digs to put the whole thing in a list. Lists were comforting when they appear to contain more reasons for a defence than you could stitch together in your head wondering around Castletown. It was simply a matter, I concluded, of *order and method*. My list was:

1)   I had had an idea to benefit my employer by putting together a brand new confection that would bring together the jam fingers that we already sold, but in a form that represents the well-known waving gesture of HRH. I called this hand, which was to be operated by battery, a *Royal Wave*.

2)   The Royal *Waves* were designed as a tribute to, and a mark of respect for, HRH and would be a way of raising the image and profile of both Candid Cakes and Castletown.

3)   I kept the idea to myself, except for *Floury Phil* and *Mechanical Mick*, who were helping me with the production side, in order to maximize the element of surprise, the jaw-dropping ingredient, if you like. Also I didn't want anyone from a rival manufacturer to steal my idea and put this product out before we did.

4)   I was going to deal with things like the *By Appointment* issue and the trademark issue when the product had been *seen* and successful at the Annual General Meeting of Candid Cakes on Monday 4th April.

5)   I really had no intention of offending anyone, least of all HRH of course!

I looked at the list with great appreciation for my own powers to mitigate the fallout from *Wave*gate, pretty hopeful that the powers that be would now understand that I was more an *innocent abroad* rather than some hardened criminal mind out to profit from stealing the royal crest or bringing it into disrepute through entirely accidental obscene hand gestures. These, after all, were purely from an accidental collision (with an idiot!) just prior to delivery of my *big idea*. I looked at the clock. This should satisfy the sandpapery lawyer. I had just enough time to call Ms

Updyke's gargantuan-breasted secretary before they closed and made an appointment. This done I sat back and penciled in 4 p.m. for the following day.

🏰 🏰 🏰

Ms Updyke had a trainee with her when I showed up for my *4 o'clock*. She was a serious, pretty red-haired girl of about eighteen or nineteen I guessed. While Ms Updyke went out to fetch her notes or resurface her face or some such, I asked the trainee what she thought of the law and this lawyer and the experience generally. She was quite talkative I found and had some quite decided views on all these subjects. I guessed that part of her legal training was capturing the questions, numbering them neatly in her head, and then ticking them off on this mental *tick list* as she delivered her answers.

"I like it here," she started off. "Ms Updyke is not the kind of lawyer, and you *do* get them, who try to paint a really rosy picture only to find that further down the line, when the client is found to be guilty, only to backtrack and start from scratch."

"Oh," I returned.

"She wants to extract the plain truth from the word go, getting all the dirty washing out in the open. Bring in a good dose of fresh air and fact. Then, when the facts are established, she *levels* with her client, tells him or her what they are up against, and that they should really *come clean*, because it would be *better for them* that way. It nearly always works out for the best. In the end Ms Updyke spends less time going round the houses and sorts it all out quickly."

"Oh I see," I returned again.

I must say this was far from music to my ears. What the pretty trainee lawyer was bringing to my mind was a picture of a crusading, scrubbed, no-nonsense legal Mary Poppins working tirelessly for the other side. I asked, "Does she ever get anybody off?"

The pretty trainee looked at me a little pityingly I thought, as though I had stumbled blindly into a world where *getting people off* was nothing short of a Utopian fantasy. She looked at the door as Ms Updyke came back into the room, bringing an air of scrubbed thoroughness and clean living with her. She looked at the trainee solicitously. This, I imagined, was just about right delivery for a solicitor. She asked, "So Helen, how are we doing?"

I considered this rather strange since *I* was the one in the *hot seat*, ready to be incinerated in a fiery ball of civic cleansing. It was as far as I was concerned, a process I could happily have lived without. So many people seemed to want me to make a clean breast of things I thought, they'd soon have me confessing to things that I'd never even thought of.

"Ms Updyke," I said.

"Yes?"

I have put together a list which I think will help show that I was only trying to do my professional duty in what transpired in the Candid Cakes Annual General Meeting. It shows I believe that I had no bad intentions in fielding my invention. I was just ... er ... trying to er ... make *Waves*." I finished off rather weakly with an unplanned pun.

I realised this was a badly constructed sentence, and left me open to attack. "What I mean by that is," I restarted.

Ms Updyke, however, was already responding to utterance number one.

"I think you've probably hit the nail on the head! Your ex-employer, Candid Cakes, have suffered a great deal of embarrassment and potential financial loss because of your antics. I think it is fair to say that they want to make an example of you. They have received a great deal of bad press over this, and we still don't know what the royal household may have to say. This all means I'm afraid, that they'll be working in harness with Castletown Trading Standards and others to make sure that the heaviest possible penalty is brought down for these offences. You have got yourself on the wrong side of a number of very influential people in the town and I think we should both be getting ready for a very rough ride indeed! This last phrase summoned up in my mind, a very personal image of Ms Updyke in a state of rugged undress that made me feel a little queasy. I came back to myself, only to hear her talking to Helen her trainee rather than to me. She sounded as though she was giving her the benefit of wisdom on a legal technicality which she would be able to make use of later in her career, should she ever meet a hardened *case* like me along the way. I was miffed at being used as a sort of laboratory rat without my permission, but she asked me at the start if it was *okay by me* if Helen *sat in,* so I couldn't really object. I looked out of the window for a moment or two until they had completed their professional analysis of my *ne'er-do-well* ways.

"You see what we have here," Ms Updyke was saying, "is a case where ignorance is no excuse in front of the law."

Helen was studiously making notes, I thought rather tastelessly, given that each word was another sharpened nail in my coffin; a coffin fashioned by Ms Updyke's no-nonsense system of admission of guilt without reference to me or, I felt, the facts! I was very tempted to ask what the expression (also used with regard to the law), *innocent until proved guilty* was *all about*, and, was there some kind of *exclusion zone* to this principle in Castletown? Ms Updyke had now finished schooling her attractive pupil and turned on me again. She huffed a little I thought.

"What I feel it would be best to do is to get a barrister appointed. I think it is very clear that this will go *all the way* and we need to put together a defence no matter how flimsy. I suggest that I look for the right man or woman for the job and give you a call in a day or two."

This said she looked at me as if she remembered the specter of fish smells in her grainy-faced expression, probably connecting it with my other cake-obscenity offence as connected flaws in my character. I left feeling that things were running a bit fast and out of control.

Chunk Eight.

Nods and Wigs

The trial was scheduled for 7th June, and I was jumpy to say the least. I was now on my way to see Ms Updyke again, this time sadly less her pretty red-headed trainee, Helen. Instead, Ms Updyke and I were joined in a crown court dungeon-chamber by a barrister, who had been appointed for me by the Crown, a Mr Vyle. The irony of the fact that the Crown had appointed *me* a barrister for a case where *I* was, in part anyway, seen to have arranged an *up yours* gesture *to* HRH (i.e. the Crown) in order to defend me *against* HRH, was not lost on me. It all played out like a strange farce of misunderstandings and mistaken identity. Shakespeare had done this trick more than a few times I thought. The two legal types present clearly hadn't spotted it though, and proceeded with *business as usual.*

"So you are (my name)?" started Mr Vyle, a much be-wigged pleasant sounding, educated man with a steady-eyed gaze. I couldn't deny it, so I nodded in agreement.

"Yes, I seem to be," I admitted simply.

He laughed lightly at this. I didn't, though, really want to *be me* at this moment. The thing was, seeing that there was no obvious way of getting out of it, I thought to myself, well, at least it's something not everyone has experienced in life. I hadn't been optimistic leading up to this much-advertised legal *bout* with *Her Maj. She* had been limbering up for some weeks now, with her trainers, *Number One* and *Spidery Woman* in her corner, wielding a range of dark superpowers and royal prerogative. I, meanwhile, in the opposite corner, would be defending myself with a dried up, somewhat mangled carcass of a *Royal Wave*, and a series of what would clearly be considered lame excuses.

"Isn't life bloody fair?" I muttered bitterly to myself.

Of course Mr Vyle and Ms Updyke were there to lend a hand. This was a mixed blessing as far as I was concerned, but I tried not to show it. We sat together, knocking our collected knees together, in the tiny floodlit cell in the bowls of the crown court discussing *tactics* and *strategy*. Mr Vyle and Ms Updyke had already been discussing my case together before I arrived they admitted. They seemed to have aligned their views into a hermetically sealed package of *final conclusions*, with which I was they implied, hopefully, going to agree quickly. They looked to see what my reaction would be to all their hard work.

"I reckon I'm buggered, don't you?" I put in as a breezy *opener*.

Mr Vyle looked a little startled at this and Ms Updyke definitely tutted.

"Well, well I don't know if it's quite *that* bad, I mean we haven't discussed our tactics regarding the hearing *of today* yet. Now let's get to it, and see if we can't come up with something shall we?"

I looked at him obliquely, and not for the first time questioned why it was necessary for people in the *professions* to slip seamlessly back in time to the language of Dickens or Austin. What was it about these huge, cavernous public buildings and the battery of officials that brought about such a strange sea-change on the brain, to come out with expressions like *let's get to it?* Clawing my way back into the 20th century I asked what I could expect from the *hearing of today* as he put it. His eyes lit up with fervour and he referred to his case notes, taking us through the *story* thus far. He studied the paperwork through round John Lennon glasses, popular at the time, all the while looking up at Ms Updyke and me for confirmations and affirmations. He said things like, *what were you intending to do with this product?* and *had you considered the probable outcome of this course of action?* He and Ms Updyke used few technical exchanges between themselves. *Tariff* was a word I heard a few times and *plea* was strewn around like confetti. It all seemed to go on for a long time and every so often a fussy legal type would poke a head round the door to see if *this room was being used* or had we seen *Judge Rogers?* Until bells and buzzers suggested that we would be needed in Court 2 in ten minutes, so please hurry up and decide if you were guilty or not. The *guilty* option was definitely the preferable to law-mongers, since it put everyone in a good mood on their side of the fence. My *Barrister-For-You* suggested if *he was me* he would be *very much inclined to consider this matter from a sensible and practical point of view*, urging me, almost begging me in fact, to *consider pleading this way,* because *one will get a third off one's sentence when the* – inevitable – *time comes.*

Ms Updyke, ever a proponent of *getting on with things* and *facing facts,* echoed Mr Vyle. They sounded so slick and synchronised. I became convinced they'd pulled this *rabbit out of a hat* together more than a few times. It was a suspicion much confirmed when they retreated a minute later with other legal types in the same fancy-dress, to a mysterious antechamber where only they could pass. I feared this was turning even nastier than I had first imagined. It did also, for the first stomach-churning time, occur to me that soon I might need to pack a toothbrush to one of these hearings! For now though, I waited for my *legal team* to emerge and advise me. They returned finally looking and sounding as though they had been deeply refreshed from a well of some elixir reserved for those in the same pantomime headgear. They were sharing a private joke, which seemed to be in pretty bad taste to me, the *condemned man sweating it out* in a room twenty inches square. I looked up as they came in. They instantly reassumed their *legal faces* and prepared, I reckoned, to deliver instructions about staying alive in the toxic antimatter world of Judge Rogers' court. However, when I looked up from my reverie I was aware that they were in fact both peering at me with looks of sympathy. This was as disturbing as it was unexpected. If there was one thing worse than being pronounced guilty *before* a trial, it's the mawkish experience of being pitied as though you have a rare and fatal medical condition. One too awful to even tell you that you had it. The moment of your doom, the looks said, is a single shrill court bell away. I shuddered inwardly at their show of faint tragic smiling and asked brusquely.

"So what's your advice?"

I could have added the word *team* I suppose but I left it. They looked at each other like parents sharing a secret sorrow and then, wordlessly elected Mr Vyle to speak for them both. He cleared his throat.

"Well, (my first name) the thing is, looking at the facts of the case, we both feel it would be best if you considered a guilty plea. It would be a practical answer to your situation, which in Ms Updyke's and my own opinion is not very hopeful."

"Not very hopeful."

Ms Updyke echoed with a tinge of sadness, as if to make sure the message couldn't be misinterpreted. "Not very hopeful."

For the second time in less than an hour I had cause to look askance and I included both *legal eagles* in the look this time. This was purely in the interests of fairness and balance, not wanting either one to feel I despised him or her over the other. It was a long time until I answered the suggestion being mooted. I was not in the mood to be wooed by their arguments and a sense of injustice had taken hold of me from some deep well-spring of my being I hadn't realised existed.

"I haven't really thought about it properly until now," I proclaimed with feeling. "But now that we *are* discussing it I don't *feel* very guilty."

I started warming to my theme now, and could sense that they were edging closer to each other, perhaps for comfort or safety. It was quite an achievement I conceded, in a room so small without actually developing an instant physical relationship. They clearly sensed a rebellion on their hands. For my part I was unrepentant and continued with my mini-rant.

"If I put in a guilty plea now, I assume I will not be able to reverse the plea later?"

Mr Vyle and Ms Updyke both nodded agreement here.

"Whereas, if I should say at this hearing that I am *not guilty* I'll be permitted I take it (I said this sarcastically and I meant it) I *will* be able to change that plea to *guilty* at a later stage?"

"Yes," Mr Vyle cut in cheerily, "but should you choose the right course *now* you will receive a third off your sentence when it comes in!"

"I see," I observed drily.

I reflected ironically that *sentences* behaved rather like trains which *came in* as reliably as the 4.25 p.m. from Paddington. Well *more* reliably, reflecting honestly on the state of the railways. I also wanted to ask if the smooth running arrival of the *Train of Justice* with its – however many – g*uilty* carriages ever came in with a *miscarriage*. It was a metaphor of my own, however, and I could see no mileage in selling it to my *one-track-minded* team. The five-minute bell went and I was urged to *decide fast*. I said, in the end, I would make my plea a *not guilty* one because, as I had indicated earlier, I didn't *feel* guilty and I hoped that the court would understand what lay behind my actions. The legal couple sighed in a resigned *on your head be it* tone and gathered their things together, all the while Mr Vyle struggling like a flightless bat with gowns and wigs and papers and the like, flapping through the corridors to our destination of Court 2, the lair of Judge Rogers. I was, despite my inner turmoil, rather intrigued to see the inside of a real court and how the legal half lived in their natural habitat. I was not to be disappointed. There was so much material in Court 2 for psychiatrists, anthropologists and other nosey types that it would have taken years to capture and catalogue in the interests of science. I sat down only to get a stern instruction that *all persons are to remain standing, if you please* until the arrival of the biggest knob in the room that day, Judge Rogers himself.

"You can be seated," boomed a fat man in a tight-fitting waistcoat.

"The Defendant will stand please," the waist-coated bursting voice said a second later making me look as though I was already out of step with procedure by trying to stand up as I was still on my way down. I obliged awkwardly and was addressed by the same voice.

"Please read out the charges against the Defendant," it commanded.

Whoever the next voice belonged to must have been a direct descendant of the man who directed poor wretches to the gallows. It sounded to me as if I was already half way there, and the *trap* I guessed was actually somewhere beneath my feet disguised by the zigzags in the parquet flooring.

"The charges are," said this new voice with the suaveness of practice. Whoever he was, he put his heart and soul into his job and hovered somewhere between actor and minor deity.

"The afore-named is charged," said the *Voice*, "that he did on or about (date) use, or cause to have used, the insignia of her royal majesty on a sweetmeat biscuit-cake product, without the requisite permissions or concessions. This is contrary to (the various Act/s etc.), and as such constitutes a contravention of (more legal stuff). The *Voice* then directed a beam of accusatory verbal limelight onto me with a specific question that could not have been side-stepped by a tap-dancer on speed.

It demanded: "How do you plead? Guilty or not guilty?" *Number One* and the *Machine* would, I speculated, have been in paroxysms of delight about this question. It was the equivalent of the hangman's noose in linguistic form. No escape from this question said the law. No escape said the Grudge, the Fury and the Witlesses. Yes or no will suffice said *Number One* and the *Machine*. Come on answer said the *Voice*.

"Guilty," I responded. A gasp of surprise would have escaped from Mr Vyle and Ms Updyke at this point, I'm sure.

🏟 🏟 🏟

Back in Castletown I wanted food. I was weary of all the legal jargon and fancied something straightforwardly greasy and comforting. I settled for *Indian Joes,* which served a *kind of* Italian food despite the contradictory name. I knew one of the waiters and could be sure of a free side order of garlic bread and fast service. I arrived at around 7.30 p.m. and immediately ordered a drink. I needed it. I looked round for Toni, the Italian waiter who I had got friendly with when he and I were both on language courses at Castletown College. I was trying to learn Italian and he English. We had both decided to *give up* together when the two respective language teachers turned out to have a combined age of around three hundred and seventy-five. It was a betting matter if they would make it to the end of the term. Toni and I went off to the pub every

Wednesday night (his night off) instead of doing the language courses, and tried teaching each other. Tonight Toni was on the till, so I didn't really get to talk to him. I was graced instead with the waitressing skills of a slim, happy Welsh girl who was also studying hairdressing at Castletown College, and waitressing to pay her way. I soon discovered the duel and entirely coincidental facts that I was really interested in hairdressing and that she had a really fantastic arse. She was interested in talking because she was bored and there were virtually no other customers. Toni was interested in talking too because she had a fantastic arse but luckily for me, he was stuck to the till. I was getting onto my second *whiskey sour* when I noticed I had gained the attention of a sweaty balding man on the only other occupied table. We two solitary customers had been strategically placed close to each other in order to foster a sense of activity for the benefit of *passing trade.* It was to suggest that tonight was not just an empty night with large helpings of lassitude and tedium on the menu. Unhappily, he seemed in the mood for conversation too; maybe he was also another instant convert to the rapidly growing fascination for hairdressing.

"Didn't I see you in Court today?" he asked out of the blue.

I felt like an ambulance driver might when, ending a day of traumatic episodes, someone collapses on top of him on his bus journey home. It was all very unwelcome to say the least. I was in mid-chat to Georgina, the Welsh waitress, who was giving me interesting hairdressing tips and pointers, and I didn't want to be interrupted by the spectre of the day that had driven me here in the first place.

"I don't recall being near a court," I cut back coldly, hoping this would put him off the scent and out of our lives forever. It didn't work. He was not of the *easily deflected persuasion*, so much so that he set about actually *moving his chair*, with a high-pitched scraping of wood on tile, over to my table and into our faces. He smiled and resumed his interruption of my doom-laden day.

"No, it was you. You're *up* for a case of using the royal crest on a cake-biscuit product. I read about it in the paper."

"Did you?" I returned blankly, "well, small world hey, now if you don't mind ..."

"Yes, *you* worked for Candid Cakes, before they kicked you out the other day. You'd set up this weird display with a hand gismo that was meant to be like the Queen's hand waving."

"Look," I tried again ...

"Yeah, that's it! Most of the fingers broke off, in fact all of them *except* the middle finger, that was left attached, and all you could see was the Queen's middle finger giving everyone the *up yours*!"

I was tired and mean by now, plus I'd had a drink. It looked to me like victimisation, and probably a *set up*. I looked at him straight in the eye. "Who are you?" I put to him bluntly.

Without batting an eyelid he stood up formally, and took my hand. "Yes, how do you do? I'm Simon Wake, chair of Castletown Round Table."

I was conscious that he said, *yes* and thought it odd. Maybe he had the idea we were trying to guess who he was, or that he was *so* well-known hereabouts that we were in a state of excitement to be introduced. I wasn't in a mood to pay homage to local dignitaries and decided that ignorance was a good way out of the encounter.

"I am sorry," I explained, "but I haven't been living near Castletown for very long and don't know anyone really except Georgina of course," I finished.

She giggled and went off to get me another drink, feeling I'm sure released from the sweaty self-importance of the good Mr Wake. He though, had other ideas about severing our new friendship and moved on with his introduction.

"I am the central plank, I suppose of the *Table*."

I thought to myself that he would actually be a *leaf* if it was a table.

He continued, "There are many important people in Castletown who contribute to the *essence* of our work, but it all passes through myself I have to say."

I was alarmed that he seemed to be warming up.

"It can become a burden to one when there are *so* many calls on one's time and so much of a need for one's opinion."

I'm stuck, I thought, in an unholy cross between a fucking Jane Austin novel and an episode of *The Prisoner*. I was playing Patrick-bloody-Darcy-McGoohan. Would it never end? I would go through this scene and then the next, thinking I had escaped, only to find that another of these inbred Castletown cronies had *tipped a wink* to the local network of shadowy criminals, bringing me full circle, back to Castletown. Now the walls of the Castle, once reassuring, were looming over me like a black turreted prison. Thankfully my drink arrived, and with it Georgina, making things a little more tolerable.

"Mr Wake," I said quickly, "I *am* sorry but I have to talk to my sister (Georgina laughed at this) before the place gets really busy. I hope you won't think me rude?"

Mr Wake was sweatily obliging at this but remarked that he hoped that my *case worked out for the best,* and that he would be sure to *check on my progress* with his contacts at the Council. He got up. *Fucking whoopee* I thought as he slipped back to the other table to get outside his own meal that had arrived in the meantime. I had another drink and scrapped the idea of food at this bar. It was after all, too full of local *characters* to relax in. Also regrettably Georgina had started to get busy with her other chores so I waved her a goodbye, paid Toni and prepared to leave. He gave me a short inquisition about my intimacy with the waitress but I shrugged it off. After all there are endless mini-encounters in life.

"It makes the world go round Toni." I added as I left, "See you Wednesday, right?"

"Yeah, bye."

I went onto Castletown Fish and Chip Shop and then, with the warm soggy bag of chips, back to my digs. I wasn't tired though and I decided it was time to fight back. I wasn't going to be *walked all over* I said to myself. I was in the middle of a list of *things to do very soon* when I fell asleep.

I woke up late again, dismayed to find that the Department of Nasty Surprises had been operating fluidly while I slumbered. Picking up my last bank statement I was disappointed to find that life wasn't as free as I'd supposed it to be. What I needed was a job and fast to avoid adding theft to my catalogue of crimes. It was entirely possible without one, I'd be thrown out of my digs and starve to death within roughly three weeks. I inwardly approved of my own alertness of mind, and decided to investigate a possible offer of work that morning. This had been made some months before by a friend of my mother's, a large quivering woman from Castletown Tourist Information Bureau. I'd go down there right now and see.

"Hello," said the Quivering Woman in question. "Yes, I certainly remember you."

This was in response to my tentative, "I don't suppose you remember me but ..."

I wasn't sure if this was a good thing or not so I determined to keep my powder dry and see how it went.

"Well, we do have some work *at the back*," QW suggested. I know (whisper) *your father* has been keen to get you *back to work* (my first name) and because of (whisper) *family connections* I will see what I can do."

I said I was grateful, which actually I was.

I went off to the job centre immediately to sign off the *dole*. I reckoned I'd been saved from the many hideous jobs they'd have allocated me. (I'd done a stint at Sloth-Town cemetery which I recounted earlier). So, although there was only one thing worse than working for QW, namely working for her at my father's behest (I'd rather do anything, to avoid it, I would go to the most outlandish ends, try anything, and work all night as a factory cleaner if necessary I kidded myself), I seemed to have run out of options. Duly, the following Monday I started at Castletown Tourist Information Bureau under QW's direction, stacking brochures and sorting out leaflets *at the back*. I felt that while the Castletown establishment was *reeling me in* like a helpless Flounder, it was nonetheless a place where I could stay solvent (just) and keep my head down. In this sense, and this sense only, it was not too bad. In every other sense it was criminally awful. QW was the most pompous person known to man. She quivered with self-importance round the clock, an achievement that would surely have brought her weight down, had she not waged a tireless campaign to keep it *topped up*. This she did by applying the *fifteen-minute rule*. This rule stated that if she hadn't *snacked* at the end of every fifteen minutes it set off an internal alarm which passed a signal to one of her staff to: *just pop out there's a love to that nice café across the road* for any one or more of the following:

1. A *nice iced bun* with *Hundreds and Thousands* (of calories) on it.

2. Two iced buns as above.

3. A *nice slice of apple pie*, with whipped cream *as standard, or I'll have to keep asking every time which makes me look a little bit greedy!* Laughs.

4. One of those *tiny* chocolate éclairs.

5. A fudge Brownie. *Okay then two, to save your poor legs!* Laughs.

Cups of tea were the standard accompaniment to each of the above. On the plus side it gave me a chance to get out of Brochure-Land and view Castletown going about its daily business. I was often on one of these errands of calorific mercy owing to QW's hypoglycemia. Thus, sadly, errands could not take too long in case she keeled over from lack of glucose. Days merged together in my mind and the only final relief was getting away at the end of the day to wander down to the river to see if the depressive waterfowl were responding to treatment, or home to my digs to think about the next stage in my *case*. These were dark days if I think back on them now, but I was a good deal younger and you can spring back more easily. It would be *okay in the end* I told myself. This would all be *wrapped up* by Christmas. Why it is necessary to do everything with reference to Christmas is pretty strange, I stopped to consider. I recall a released hostage saying on TV once that when you are chained to a radiator in a windowless room for six years in a nameless hellhole somewhere, Christmas is a real bummer. The rest of the time presumably was a stroll in the park! Perhaps, I speculated, it would have been kinder of their captors to have skipped the festive period altogether, thus avoiding the heightened anguish of missing mince pies and brandy butter! They were probably somewhere in the Muslim world anyway I speculated, where Christmas was not really their *big thing*. I was still dwelling on the privations of a non-festive hostage situation when there was a knock on the door. I wasn't a big fan of knocks on doors at the time. They meant either, a) *Keep the bloody music down you hippy xxxx*, b) *Where's this month's rent, you hippy xxxx?* Or c) *Can I borrow your kettle you hippy xxxx?* That I wore my hair over the collar was a matter of personal choice, but a crime against humanity for my landlord, Mr

Givall. I wanted this to be a *kettle request* rather than the rent because money had been tight over the last couple of weeks. I was not exactly flush. The door opened, I looked half relieved and half surprised to see Georgina from *Indian Joes*. She smiled and asked if I was going to *leave her on the step like a bottle of milk*. This hadn't occurred to me as an option so I simply asked her in. She clearly could see no obstacle so in she came, *really nice* arse and all. I guess I hadn't thought about sex or love or any related topic for ages now. I wasn't aware of how long I hadn't until Georgina got very close to me and said she was *worried about me* and had decided to come over and see *how I was*. It was then *precisely*, that *I* realised how worried I also was about me. She said she was *sorry for me* too. Uncanny is the only word for it because, I felt exactly the same way myself about me. She really had a gift for extrasensory perception, this pretty Welsh girl with the really nice rear. She was on my wavelength and no mistake, she even wanted to *help make me feel better* she said. I said *yes you must*! So she did.

After Georgina had made me feel better twice, I was so much better and also totally exhausted. Of course I explained that I was *not out of hot water yet*, and would love to see her again soon. She said she had to go home to make some supper for her mum who had been left a widow when her father accidentally ran himself over with a tractor while mending it. Apparently he had not secured the handbrake or whatever tractors have. I didn't laugh at this (as it would have been in very poor taste) until she closed the door. I hoped she hadn't heard me. A second earlier (in a tender moment as she was leaving) she'd made me promise to make *her* feel better (about this family tragedy, even though it was ten years ago) and could I do this tomorrow at the same time?

"Yes I can!" seemed the only polite response.

"But let me call you when I know my rota at the tourist office."

She agreed readily, clearly seeing me for the upstanding youth I was, acting purely out of kindliness and concern. After she'd left I slept soundly for a time, then went to see if the ducks were okay. They were all fine as far as I could tell, though spotting signs of psychosis in ducks wasn't my special area. Eventually I went home and to bed early in order to wake up fresh to another day of brochures, leaflets, and lifesaving sugar-runs. It was tedious but it paid the bills and I wasn't in a position to move onto anything else for the time being. I did want to get the court case out of my hair though, so I was actually relieved in a way when I got the trial date in the post the next morning. It would be three months away (Friday September 3rd) which seemed like a very long time to have it hanging over my head. What could I do to keep my mind off it until then? Georgina was the answer that came into my head almost without any hesitation. I decided to call her the moment I got back.

Georgina looked lovely with her hair freshly washed and her fantastic rear dressed in a tiny, clingy skirt. She was a heaven sent relief from my troubles of the mind. I wondered why god bestowed such bounty on the young and then (we discover later in life) whips them neatly away like the cruel omnipotent conjuror he is. Still at this time I *was* one of the young, and determined to enjoy my time while the going was good. The going, as it happened, was firm to hard and we *got going* as soon as we could, as often as we could. The landlord, Mr Givall, gave me strange looks these days that I deciphered as a mix of suspicion and envy. I avoided him as much as possible on this pretext now, as well as the usual ones of music, rent, and kettles. It was an odd time but it passed, and I found myself nearing the case date before I knew it. In fact when I looked at my diary I breathed in with a sharp jolt, *shit that's next Wednesday, next week, my god, next fuuuucking week*! This necessitated my acting in some focused way, to come up with something in the way of a plan and a means of execution. It was not what I would have called a relaxed day after that. Some little while after Georgina had left for her *shift* at *Indian Joes*, I wended my way to the river, settling on my usual bench near the still down-hearted ducks. I went through the statements from the prosecution I'd brought with me, sharing the bag of stale bread for the waterfowl.

Chunk Nine.

Crime and Prejudice

The statements were ghastly, really, consisting of a concerted effort to have me *swing*. I was certain that a nasty email must have done the rounds among those who were *out to get me.* I didn't have far to look since their names were all there in black and white. What I figured though, was that they were just the tip of a murky iceberg of gits who wanted me out of Castletown and probably thought it better if I was dead too. It was amazing, I also mused, that so many people who I didn't know and whom I had never met; never would meet, hated me so much.

"It is in the nature of things," opined Mr Vyle. "There's something in all of us that wants to *hurt* his fellow man. Much of it is down to casually malign feelings rather than substantive facts. Some of it is bound to *stick* though, if you know what I mean?"

I knew exactly what he meant.

"No I meant *mud* Mr (my name). We try to use, well *politer terminology* when addressing clients, or in court, don't you know?"

I was again struck by language *washing up* from some sepia-tinted past era, but suggested to him that *in the end* what it meant was I'd *have the book thrown at me, right?*

His position on this was that he *didn't necessarily agree,* and to give him his legal escapologist's due, he didn't really disagree either. He was better than any politician I reckoned and made a real art-form out of both not committing himself whilst coming up with one nightmare scenario after another, adding quickly after it, *but that may not happen of course.* I was no better off when I left him for the last time before I was hauled up in front of the *beak.* But of course there were others to be thought about bubbling up in the unholy judicial cauldron. There were various witnesses (*witlesses*). They really did bother me.

111

They were people I'd met, characters comprising the very fabric of Castletown. Much worse than this, they were part of the *same piece of fabric* of Castletown. If you annoy one of them you annoy them all. The *fabric* was a continuous wrap-around, which brought Castletown folk into a *close-knit*, stifling *group hug* of outraged civic duty. They were eager to cut out any rotten part of their prized core and spit it as far away from them as possible. In this case, *I* was that rotten *core* and they were clearly preparing to chew me up and spit me out! It was an unappetizing thought that haunted me until I met up with Georgina again later that evening at the Castletown Wine Bar.

"Next Wednesday."

I gloomily answered Georgina's question. I was in the habit of *playing it up* with her now because she was a motherly type, underneath an anything-but-motherly frame, and her sympathy had a wonderful outlet in comforting the needy in ways that I found agreeable and regular.

"You *poor thing*!" Georgina cooed, putting her hand on my leg for moral support.

"Shall I come and watch?"

Now I hadn't considered this until she asked, and I had to think carefully before answering. I didn't want to offend her but equally I wasn't at all sure that I wanted her there either.

"Let me think about it," I delayed.

"Okay, let me know," she suggested cheerfully, in no way thrown by my answer.

She was a great girl with a perfect posterior. I was a lucky guy. Some girls I knew would have bridled the second you didn't immediately say *yes*, but *Georgie* was just so relaxed and didn't mind either way. Brilliant I thought and forgot about it completely and forever. It wouldn't have been her kind of thing anyway, I argued to myself. She was more a part of my good times and this dark day didn't need to get her down. I just hoped I would make it back to her comforting arms at the end of it!

"It will be a two-dayer I think," pronounced Mr Vyle on the phone in my *last minute advice for clients'* call.

"I would be prepared for long days too. This Judge Rogers is a bit of a stickler for procedure I understand."

This was bad news. Anyone who is described as a *stickler* is automatically dogmatic and probably despotic I reflected. This struck the fear of god into me from that moment on. Mr Vyle added before he rang off, that *if he was me he'd read and re-read the prosecution statements and familiarize himself with the central planks of his own defence. Planks*, I reflected with an ironic expulsion of air, to be *walked* no doubt, and full of woodworm and splinters. I was on a worm-infested splintery plank on a doomed ship of my own construction, heading into choppy, unknown waters. Navigation was not my strong point. Anyway I was ready for a fight. After all, I really had not intended any harm. I sat down with a cup of Horlicks and got to work on re-reading the nasty prosecution statements. Bedtime reading it wasn't. The first one was the statement from a woman called Ms C Agitess (a-gitess was nearer the mark) from Candid Cakes legal department, who *went to town* on the matter of unauthorized use of the

Candid Cakes' name and the *negative effect* of the debacle on public opinion re Candid's image in the industry and beyond. She focused on various newspapers, quoting some of the *bad press* that my antics had attracted. She quoted the paper as saying, which I had read myself of course, that the whole affair had *linked Candid Cakes in the public's mind with a slur on HRH*. She implied people would not buy products, which were *tainted by association* with this obscene act. It was almost, she wrote, *tantamount to treason*. Next up was *Floury Phil* and, to be fair, he simply put things as they were. He didn't seek to blacken my name and said it as it was. I figured that his statement would be a simple case of recorded fact without any *side* to it. The same for *Mechanical Mick* although he did say (with intonation) he *had* warned me about use of the royal crest. I reckoned it wouldn't have done him any harm to have left this out. Again, aside from this, it was a pretty straightforward record of the exciting early days of *Royal Waves;* thinking them up and baking them into existence. Sadly, now was the time for explaining their purpose and recording their demise. I did, somewhere within me though, nurture the hope that they could rise again from the blackened baking tray of fate. Next up were the horrors of *Spidery Woman* and *Number One*. I'd been through this once and could really do without revisiting it. However, I knew I had to *mug up* on this stuff before I was due in Court 2 on Wednesday. On this day it would be festooned with grudge-bearing Judge Rogers and his band of merry gaolers. It was, though, the testimony of the two above that really put me out. They'd no firsthand knowledge of what had gone on, preferring a *one-size-fits-all* approach to wrongdoers and ne'er-do-wells. This convenient self-assembly *justice kit* could be *put together* in nice neat pre-numbered sections, ensuring a superb *guilty finish*. With the help of *little pieces* of legal dogma (supplied) the final product could be rushed along to the Judge (the Grudge) to present to the court. *Spidery Woman* had helpfully written a grim condemnatory line or two focusing on what happened during my processing at Castletown Trading Standards HQ along with details about *offering Mr (my name) refreshments, which he accepted.* Then there were a series of lines about what they'd asked me and what I'd said in response. No mention was made of her tiny help-meet on the ceiling and I assumed she wanted to keep his/her identity a secret. There were no further surprises in the statements except that *Number One* made a long tedious aside about *we at Castletown Trading Standards are conscious of our duty and responsibility to make sure that nobody misappropriates or misuses any insignia (royal or otherwise) for the purpose of* ... etc. etc. I couldn't bring myself to go on any more for now so I shelved the statements and went out. I reckoned I should have enough of a basis for defending myself now on the *big day.* My own defence was really centred on the: *I did not mean to do it* school, which I thought might *swing it* for me if the jury were nice, honest, upstanding maternally inclined, elderly women with loveable and roguish sons of their own!

Chunk Ten.

The Grudge, the Fury & the Witlesses

It is important to keep in mind I think, that the exposure of a person's *guilt* is often merely an accident of timing. How many guilty people still await such exposure, or elude it forever, or at the least during their lifetimes? Guilt is one of those phenomena that only become *real* once brought into the light of day. While guilt lurks in the shadows it is invisible to the eye, and while its owner stays still, it remains inside the margins of his own shadow. Only when light is shone on the subject does the guilty shadow become visible to the rest of us. Plato would have approved of this theory I reckon.

The judge was vengeful; a retired dictator I guessed. The jury was in a fury at being *kept in at playtime,* and the witnesses, well, witless. Judge Rogers, or *Grudge Rogers* as he was more affectionately known, presided over his court like a giant irritable, dipsomaniac baby with a gavel-shaped rattle. It was going to be a disaster and I was already summoning up images of cells, slopping out, and dark deeds in the showers. It was a nasty jolt. The world of comfy chairs by the fire seemed to be dodging backwards like a tiny spec on a platform when the train pulls out. My old life I told myself gloomily was soon to become a distant memory, and a world of bumping into the wrong kind of fellow-inmate about to materialize. I turned my attention to the procedure of the court. At present I was standing waiting for the charges to be read out in pin-dropping silence. It was as if someone had died but we hadn't been given the *s.p.* on whom. I was only aware that nobody was really *on my side.* Even my own *team* had begun to display strange allegiances with all the other legal fancy-dressers. The whole of Court 2 seemed to be configured in a feudal arrangement of *chosen ones* looking down on unfortunates who had fallen into a legal *pit* at their feet. Judge Rogers finally entered to hushed silence. He was on a dais so high that we all got neck ache just looking up at him. All normal rules of life had flown out of the window and the court *time-machine*, something like the *Tardis*, had landed on an alien landscape where the life forms spoke in a language that mimicked our own but was actually quite different. The customs were strange too.

Some of the inhabitants of *Courtworld* chose to wear strange clothes. These ones spoke in very loud voices and addressed the man in a cloak and odd headgear on the dais. When they spoke to the god-figure they bowed forward as a ritual of, I imagined, respect and said things with a distinct insinuation that they would be very happy to lick his boots, and probably other zones too. He spoke in a loud voice, but not politely. In fact, he grunted and snarled quite a lot and when one of his *worshipers* made a mistake or even when they didn't, he snapped at them like a piranha in a cape. He was some kind of god clearly. He had servants as well as worshipers. These were sitting quite close to him and occasionally gave him offerings of paper or whispered abasements into his grizzled ears. He was, throughout all of this, uniformly bad-tempered and demanding. If something didn't happen instantly and or to his taste, he would look over his perched spectacles and wither his correspondent like fast acting weed killer. He was a creature with a very simple outlook; do everything I want you to do. Do it correctly and instantly, or you perish horribly. I marvelled at how smoothly this highly balanced system ran. There wasn't a single dissenting voice in the place, and I imagined all on that side of the *line* were really happy with it. I, on the other hand, would have changed a number of things I conjectured. I would have made the law a little less of a slick *courtroom to choky processing plant*. Maybe I could flag up my objection to the school of *that's just how things are*, or object to the irascible being presiding from his throne. He was though, clearly so prone to flying into a rage if his arse wasn't instantly wiped by his team of geriatric nurses, that I stalled. I mused over how court *arrangements* had been conceived to make you look like a tiny insect-like criminal. You were obliged to hold yourself ready at all times for figurative decapitation just for misunderstanding what was expected of you. You were judged, from that moment and forever, in the light of your stultifying ignorance of court practices and failure to grasp the *rules of engagement*. Then you had an appointment to be mauled by a series of belligerent *groupies* from the opposition who already had you labelled as the antichrist. They only needed, I sensed, a few moments of time in front of the irascible *Supreme Being* on the dais to prove this *beyond all reasonable doubt*. The air was full of the kind of expectation bloodhounds enjoy so much on Saturday mornings. The Dais Team was looking down especially disdainfully. I reckoned these were the last minutes of my freedom ticking away. They called the first witless witness. It had to be *Spidery Woman*. I thought to myself only her optimism and light-heartedness were called for to make this a really fun day. It was. *Spidery Woman* had undergone a minor transformation. Instead of her black spidery hippy gear, she had on a suit. It was as though she had metamorphosed into a black moth and taken to the air. Her demeanour was not happy or uplifted but it was more animated and business-like. She stood in the appointed place and read from a laminated card that stuff about telling the truth; non-God version. This didn't surprise me in the least since I already knew she was part of a coven of insect worshippers and indeed one of the undead. I waited while various facts relating to name, address and the like were ploughed through until, grudgingly the *Supreme Being* was happy with it all. She was asked about our council meeting *under caution* with (my full name). She went fairly repetitively through all the stuff that we already know about. She recited various laws and their many sub clauses about trademarks, insignia etc. that seemed much more interesting to everyone but me. She was quite red-cheeked and exhilarated when she stepped down at the end of it all.

Then *Number One* had his shot at it. He also did the ever popular Return of the Taped Interview Show. This was now a classic, featuring me coming into the interview room, being taped while I was offered a cup of tea, masquerading as *refreshments* only to be interrogated in front of the *Machine*. I looked carefully at *Number One,* having a sneaking suspicion that he may have smuggled the *Machine* into court as a promised treat. It didn't appear this way though since he was a tall lean man, and couldn't really have anything more than six or so pens on his person in the way of official weaponry. He had a go at reciting the laws and clauses thing too. It seemed to go down well with the various arrayed ranks of prosecutors. Faint smiles were exchanged. Mick and Phil had obviously clubbed together to hire a couple of cheap suits from Moss Bros. They looked uncomfortable in this alien world too. We exchanged embarrassed looks across the room. Then in came a bigger boss from Castletown Trading Standards. He confirmed to the SB that what his inferiors were saying was in fact true, but that he would tell us again anyway. Judge Grudge seemed to like this line of attack because to the legally trained I guessed it must have been corroborating opinion or some such. He would have learned all about this in the days when he was being dipped in caustic soda, or whatever they used, to *toughen judges up* for locking up the criminal classes. I looked at my watch, as I did so a voice proclaimed that we should *all stand* because the SB needed a sufficient degree of awe while going out for his din-dins.

We all filed out and went to places where you can go to be stared at by others from both sides of the divide; the punishers and the punished. I went to a bleak cafeteria on *level 4* and decided not to eat a whole meal but have something sweet as an energy boost for my upcoming bloodbath in the afternoon. I spotted a Candid Cakes woman across from me with a disarmingly large bundle of papers, all of which I felt must mention me without very much affection. She was having a *proper meal* of pasta with salad. I felt sick and went to get some fresh air, *while I still could* I thought grimly. The afternoon was warm for September and a few birds did their best to get me to look on the bright side by chirruping encouragingly. It didn't really work. I toyed idly for a minute or two with thoughts of escaping to France or Spain on a ferry. A romantic day-dream doomed to failure by that bastard *Practicality*, and his half-sister (also outside wedlock) *Common-Fucking-Sense*. It was with a heavy heart that I climbed the steps back into the huge sprawling stone building again. I knew I had to put on a good performance if I was going to see the light of day without a vulgar *bar motif* constantly getting in the way. All in all it was the longest day of my life but I had word from Vyle that actually it will be a mere *one-dayer* after all. The arguments he explained are *quite clear-cut*. I was amazed that the arguments which he had been conjuring with like a deranged alchemist were now *quite clear cut after all*. This meant that since I hadn't packed a toothbrush the spectra of jail-issue grooming products was also upon me. These would be made from recycled matches and cigarette papers of course. I went to sit down in the reconvened other world of Court 2 when we were all jerked back to frenzied forelock tugging by the loud voice of an official who advertised the arrival of the Supreme Being, Judge (Grudge) Rogers. I speculated whether he had been mellowed by a good meal and a gallon of the finest port. I was to be disappointed. He looked, if anything, as though someone had slipped a slug into his salad and spat into his beer. I faced ahead until I was called upon to take the stand.

The Judge's *summing up* was next on the menu so I braced myself for the inevitable bad news. I thought of Georgina who would have just loved to sooth my fevered brow at this moment. A bit of brow-soothing was definitely called for in the pregnant atmosphere of Court 2. Judge Grudge, the Fury and the Witlesses, witless as they all looked, were clearly relishing the moment. They anticipated my imminent and needless to say entertaining flattening into a very thinly extruded byproduct of the legal machine. It was a bad moment. I looked straight ahead as all condemned men are expected to do. It wouldn't be long now. I listened to the Supreme Being running over my heinous crimes just once again for the general delectation of the crowd and stressing the indignity done to the image of HRH too. It was, he implied, especially galling that Castletown, of *all* towns, should be involved in such a case! He was nearly roused to emotion on this last point and the only thing missing was a tear of outraged chivalry in defence of that fragrant personage herself. *They're going to throw the fucking book at me* I murmured under my breath. I was waiting for it to be thrown. *Judge Grudge* was *bringing down* his sentence and the w*itless witnesses* and the f*urious Jury* were all holding their various breaths as to the outcome. I wasn't sure if my breath was actually operating at all at this point, and the world seemed to spin off its axis and trot across space under its own steam. I was a man without any hope. The vast ungodly landscape of the courtroom, Court 2, was acting out a time-honoured tradition of meting out justice, handing it down and letting it fall on the selected head. In this case it was my head, which had been selected, and I wasn't happy about it. I waited forever and then a little longer. The time passed and the catalogue of my misdeeds got longer and longer. I was surprised to hear that not only had I transgressed laws that had their very own categories, but also others that were related, by some rare genetic fluke to them, and this actually *doubled* the tally of my crimes. The hushed courtroom was now ready for the final verdict; everyone was hushed and respectful.

"The series of events initiated by (my name)," pronounced *Judge Grudge,* "have had far-reaching and negative effects not only on Candid Cakes, the firm that took you on (my name), but also have been of grave and serious detriment to the name of the British monarch. In view of the very offensive character of the events which transpired because of your actions, I have to weigh various factors in the balance. I accept that you are young and perhaps that your overall intentions were not to bring about the outcomes that they did bring about. You are a man of good character ... (I didn't misinterpret this because Mr Vyle had explained that this simply meant they hadn't *done* you before) and I imagine that you still have it in you to turn your life around and become a good citizen. However, there must be a penalty for this behaviour that reflects the seriousness of the misdemeanours committed. I feel that a custodial sentence is warranted, which I will suspend for twenty-four months. The sentence I pass then is forty weeks suspended. I also order that you do one hundred and fifty hours of community service unpaid and for the good of society. I do hope (my name) that you learn a lesson from this trial and that I never have to see you before me again."

He didn't add ... *and may god have mercy upon your soul* but it wouldn't have sounded out of place.

I realised I hadn't actually passed out, but when he had started the first part of his sentence but had not quite (as he would one millisecond later) reached the second part of it, my world already in the *oh-my-sweet-Christ-sphere*, suddenly screamed into warp factor sixty, bolting out to where no man has gone-be-fucking-fore. I came back to the jolly green planet though with a little more sanity when he did finally add the line about "suspended for twenty-four months". He did of course spoil the thing with some bad news about community service. Even so it was a relief on a scale that I couldn't have imagined. One moment I was sharing a virtual cell with mass-murderers, gangsters and rapists, and the next I was out in the emerald green grass drinking in lashings of good clean air. I left the court after having passed on details relating to my community service order and almost skipped home. Castletown looked its most beautiful as my train pulled in. Also, I was meeting Georgina for a drink and a shag. Technically speaking I may not have mentioned the second part specifically but it was pretty much a *given* as Americans say. The day, having started out really badly was ending much better than I had feared, and I even got an official job out of it as a bargain. I didn't spend any of my time pondering what this might be since it belonged to a different tense of life called the *future uncertain continuous*. Like young people every-where, I was simply living for now!

Chunk Eleven.

Making Molehills out of Mountains

I have always subscribed to the theory that there is a cunning *law* in human nature that allows for the minimizing of – sometimes significant – negatives by making light of them in your own mind. This renders them less awful and thus easier to cope with. Let's call this law: *Making molehills out of mountains*. This is, by the way, a close relation to the law of: *Getting away with it*. It is a law much favoured by the young, and holds that if you have been *getting away with it* (whatever it is that you have been getting away with for a long time, maybe most of your life) by the time you get to a point, perhaps later in life, and you haven't actually been caught, you should put a full stop to doing whatever you're doing. This is based on the reasoning that you've actually been *bastard lucky* up to this point, and if you continue *pushing your luck*, you will almost certainly run out of it. In short, quit while you're ahead! It was a good law, and even though I didn't exactly feel guilty about what had got me into these recent scrapes, I decided to adopt the principles of the above law in my life from some point in the middle future. That would be then, of course.

For now, as the time turned 8-ish a.m. I set off to start my first half-day of community service as decreed by *Judge Grudge*. Surely it wouldn't be that bad. It would be a case of making the most of it according to the *molehills out of mountains law*. I turned up at the back of a small factory unit five miles from Castletown to report to *Ron*. I found that indeed it was much better than it might have been. Ron was cheerful and direct. I would be responsible for testing/mending small pieces of electrical equipment. Toys and radios, torches and watches were my *job* and I could sit down to do it. Sitting down on the job from the start, smart! – As we said at the time.

"We usually get them younger than you," he started conspiratorially.

I looked questioning.

"Well you know, D&D, TWOC, etc."

I didn't know so he had to tell me. *TWOC* was, I learned, *Taking a vehicle Without the Owner's Consent* and *D&D*, I should have been able to work this one out for myself, drink driving.

"So what are you *in* for?" Ron enquired with good old-fashioned directness that I liked.

"How long have you got?" I asked him.

Over the following three weeks and beyond, I told Ron and the others, who I got to know at the factory unit, about the affair of the *Royal Waves*, about how it all went wrong and how I ended up there as well as my other job at Castletown Tourist Information. I went through the various *chapters* of my story about Castletown Trading Standards and my *legal team* and how the law looked from my point of view. We grew in camaraderie as they gave me back some stories they had to relate about the same legal system and way things often really *worked out* once you had stripped away what your parents told you about life. The group I was working with, Ron himself, June, and Linda (Lin) all had their stories to tell. It was a real education as the expression goes. Lin was a lovely tender hearted woman of about sixty, losing her husband to bowel cancer. It was obviously deeply painful for her but she somehow managed to keep connected with other people and steer away from melancholy. I liked her a great deal and she always managed to smuggle me something nice from the canteen when they took their lunch. I was to make *my own arrangements* in line with the rules of my *order*. This also stated that I was not to be entrusted with any *cash or valuables*. This was a nice archaic touch I thought. I looked over the paperwork for the clause that said I should also be *shackled and whipped periodically*.

"So Lin what did you do before this?"

She smiled and stayed silent for quite a while and I was worried I may have offended her. It wasn't the case though, because I could see that she was just more inclined to put things to me in her own way, which meant a few minutes of deliberation.

"Well, you see I'm Romany," she started off.

It was the beginning of November. I was regularly walking into work at the tourist office and then walking on afterwards, or beforehand depending on the day, to the factory unit. In short, I was doing a great deal of walking, which as all walkers know, gave me time to think. I thought about *the nature of things* as my barrister put it. The *nature of things* I concluded was all to do with how you *play it*. It was clear that some people deal with life quite differently from others. For a start, this experience of social punishment was an eye-opener and had proved a huge and surprising bonus to my spirit. If the truth be told though, there was not one iota of regret in me about what had led to it, nor any sense of *paying back* anything to society. Society in any event, follows a system known technically as *dodging and weaving,* coupled with its sister activity of *ducking and diving*. When I first went to the unit I realised that most people *get by* in life and coming as I did from a *nice middle class* background, I had been completely oblivious to what went on in the real world. People were fundamentally okay I thought, basically kind. What became clear was that this essential kindness was also contingent on what – often huge – pressures were working to make their lives less comfortable. External pressures forced some very gritty outcomes on some very kindly folk. I was certainly not there, I told myself, to judge anyone; after all they didn't judge me. I was *in* with them as I never could have been if I had come via another route. The set-up at least gave me a canvass to redraft parts of myself and *hear* things I hadn't been open to before. It is, as the superb playwright Edward Albee, once said: "Sometimes it is necessary to go a long way out of the way in the wrong direction in order to come back to the right place." I had arrived here at this unit, and to these conclusions, by a path I couldn't have started to guess at a few weeks before. The hugeness of the judgement now seemed not only a lesser event than it had at the moment of its delivery; it seemed like a blessing, albeit heavily disguised. What I had thought to be mountains of worry turned in reality, to be molehills on the *road of experience*. I saw even more clearly from this point, that life was about how you viewed it. As someone once said (I forget who): *It's not the situation, but how you see the situation*. All in all, I came to see the factory as a more interesting place than Castletown proper. I really missed going there when my time was up.

The hard facts are the hard facts though, and I realised I would have to somehow get a new job, and one *with prospects* (as my parents always put it) when the time came. For now I was in the bosom of a newfound family of equals, and I liked it. Gradually the days holding off the *festive season* as it is perhaps (for some) ironically termed, slipped away, as I continued to mend small toys and put batteries in watches. I renewed the faces of clocks and *PAT* tested everything from the light bulbs to (and including) the kitchen sink. I made *proper* tea with six sugars for Ron, and no sugar for Lin and poured endless mugs of Diet Coke for June. The unit was a retreat and a sanctuary from the hassle of the tourist information bureau, and a resting place after being mothered and *comforted* by Georgina. This continued as a pattern right up until she dropped out of Castletown College and went off to do a foundation course in Sheffield – and that was that. I didn't really mind since we were both at an age where having given of ourselves to each other selflessly, often several times a night, we moved on. This code between the young is healthy and strings loose. We said we would meet at Christmas knowing it wasn't true, and parted happy. I had, by my reckoning, another three months of *community service* to do, so I settled in quite happily to the work and looked around for something to do when my *time* ran out. I would look seriously after Christmas I told myself. Christmas is always a line in the sand and in the mind. It was surprising to me then that I was offered a job interview at a large merchant bank before Christmas with a view to becoming a stockbroker's errand boy. I could then, as the theory goes, work my way up to the position of *fat cat* in no time. I would see what it was all about I told myself. I learned that the surprise interview was in reality actually some *string-pulling* in the family. I would go anyway though I resolved. It couldn't hurt. I wouldn't have to sell my soul, I thought, I'd just *see*.

The interview was to take place at a restaurant in the West End. It was a while since I had been to London and even longer since I had been on the *consumption end* of a restaurant. I *had* worked at a few two summers before, as a washer-upper, but this was an exciting departure. I was to meet with two top *people* at the bank, Warlock, Banter and Steep (I think). I was ready for the appointment five hours ahead of schedule, but told myself I could *mug up* on banking and bankers on the train up. Ron was great, he intervened for me with the Punishment Department to get me the afternoon off to prepare and get to town by no later than 6 p.m. to be absolutely ready for 7.30 p.m., the time of the dinner-meeting with the firm of merchant bankers. I was meeting a mysterious pair called *Molly and Dolly* my brother told me. Now this sounded like a really odd combination until I had possession of their full names. I was met at the door to the restaurant by Martin Mollier and Dorian Dolitus. They were really smart. They wore smart clothes, had smart brains, and made smart comments. After an hour with them, I concluded I had been very sheltered in every way up to that moment. We ordered *whatever you want* from the menu, which was Greek. Dorian Dolitus was the more senior of the two and of Greek extraction, so he spoke intelligently about the menu and offered me good advice, which I took. He also ordered wine, but chose *French wine;* smilingly indicating *it beats Greek.* We started off talking about everything from Greece to girls, sometimes combining the two. *"Greek girls,"* he told me with an arch smile, "were *like the Aegean; warm and wet."*

We laughed and drank a great deal more wine of both the red and white flavours. The conversation didn't really adopt a more serious tone until the time honoured Greek tradition of throwing large dinner plates around the restaurant arrived. It was a dramatic moment in the evening and I thought *Molly* and *Dolly* as I had been encouraged to call them seized this moment to test my metal. It could conceivably have been anything from tin foil to toughened steel. They let me throw a few plates and each time they picked one up themselves they posed a question with a kind of wild energy attached to it.

"So, why do you want to make huge sums of money and shag lots of beautiful girls?"

I thought this just must be a trick question. But the more I thought about it the more I realised there was only one answer.

"What guy doesn't?" I asked.

I was pleased to see the virtual score board in their faces registering a tick here.

"Your brother says you had a bit of a scrape with the Law?"

Dolly's question threw me somewhat I must say. But *Dolly* and *Molly* were already ahead of me.

"Look, this game's all about ambition. If you really did what your brother *says* you did, if anything it makes you *more qualified* to do the job than less," *Molly* concluded.

"*Some people* may see it as a problem or an obstacle, but what it actually shows is you've got balls; and so long as you don't get caught, we need that kind of mentality. See yourself as a mountaineer. It's dangerous work, daring work, not for the fainthearted. The thing is to never slip, never fall, because in this game that would be very far indeed and extremely painful. As things stand your past is a mere pinprick on the horizon, onward and upward my boy, onward and upward!"

I was quite gaggingly happy to hear this. In my brain, there was a struggle going on though. While the Spiritual Growth Division was unhappy, the Irresistible Temptations Section was all for it. I decided for the present to allow ITD to overrule SG. I argued that for now they should work as a team, chiefly because a long lost friend, Monetary Gain, was sorely needed back in my life! The evening went on and the plate smashing event gave way to more conversation. Plans were made to have me *come into the office* on the following Monday, *just to do some basic numeracy tests, nothing major, shouldn't be a big deal.*"

Thus spake *Molly* and *Dolly*.

I failed the numeracy test miserably of course. In fact from the very second of the casual aside over dinner about the numerical testing, I realised the glittering package of money, success and beautiful women was in the bin. They didn't know what I knew, namely that I quite simply couldn't add up to save my life. Chalk it up to experience I told myself, as I looked for a job in the local paper the week after Christmas. The Greek goddess fantasy having fled, life had settled down again into the same pattern. I had two months of community service left and I would be unshackled and let loose with a clear conscience, back into society. The question was still though, what to do. I was talking to my father at some point and he (wily old fox that he was) came to my rescue. On the basis of eliminating all the things that I couldn't do (a long list) he whittled it down to what, as he put it, I could *get away with before I was found out*. His dry humour was always a support. He dug out a *small ad* from the local paper and passed it over to me. It read, *Entrepreneurs required for novel franchise opportunity. Start-up investment £5000.* I looked at it with some interest but flagged up an obvious problem. Where am I going to get the money? My father looked in one of his sunnier moods and said he had *been thinking about that* and that he would *see me okay* on the investment. I was really excited and grateful and I said so. I didn't think you would ever give me money for this kind of thing I said. He looked over with his ironically amused face.

"I am not going to give you any money."

He explained further. "I shall make an overdraft arrangement for you at the bank, and you will have that money to start with, then you will have to pay it back as you go and grow."

Well this didn't actually dampen my spirits too much as I figured that, since it was at his suggestion, and he was putting his name to the debt, I would be *in the clear* if it went *tits up* anyway. I didn't say this at the time. He was kind but gruff, my father, belonging to a gruff old school outlook of hard fought success in life, gained through adversity. He was though, always on a hairspring of irritability towards stupidity. He – sometimes subtly – *laid into* those not on his intellectual plain. There were few who came up to scratch. But I was his son of course, and sons are different; they got the same fierce judgement but could always turn up at the door for more chances. Others were not so lucky. I kissed my darling mother and went back to my digs with the promise from my father that he would *set it all up* and that I should hear from the bank soon. I was pretty happy about all of this. Since my recent biscuit-related fall from grace had been very much to do with trying to start something up I was pleased by his faith in me. The challenge excited me; I was very keen to get this started and *make a go of it*.

Chunk Twelve.

Myths, Gargoyles and Google-Ghoul

The start-up of the (as it transpired) gourmet birdseed franchise, was to be in early April. Why birds would want gourmet seed, and how anyone knew they could tell the difference with bog-standard seed, was unclear to me. This meant that my last visit to the factory unit would be just before this as it fell just prior to Easter. I would be sad to leave the unit, Ron, Lin and June, but then it was sadness offset by the excitement of starting the franchise. The first thing had been to see the bank manager, an event in every young man's life that sticks in the memory forever. The man I would see was a Mr A Bandon and he had dealt with my father for over thirty years. Mr Anthony (not that I would be using his first name) Bandon was an *old-school* bank manager with a gentle fatherly way about him. He viewed me I thought, when we met, as a – probably – errant young tearaway (like all young men) who wanted to take the bank's money and spend it as quickly as possible. This was both perceptive and accurate. He started off. "£5000 is a great deal of money."

He sounded as though he was schooling a shark about turning vegetarian. His tone was encouraging but had the suggestion that, if I went back to being a meat-eater, he also had recourse to an electric prod for the purpose of *correction*.

"Money," the bank manager continued, "is not what people think it is …" He looked at the bank's ceiling as if for inspiration from a higher authority. Perhaps in banking terms this would be the Bank of England I pondered.

"Money," his emphasis and enthusiasm increasing, "is *not* for spending!"

"Money," (he paused and stared meaningfully at me) "is *opportunity; opportunity and timing*. What most young men tend to do when they get … er, a *facility like this* is to see before them *goods and services*. What they *should see*, what *you* should see, is opportunity and timing!"

I was quite keen to defend my honour but thought maybe my father had already warned him about me so left the slur undefended for now.

"You," (he peered at me intently over his glasses, kindly but accusingly) "see a car perhaps, because you argue to yourself that a car would be *very nice* (his tone scoffed at the words) to get you to places to pick up items for this new venture and thus it would make sense."

Now he was talking my language. He seemed to be reading my mind and put in quickly and sharply, though still fatherly in tone. "Now my boy, this is exactly what money is *not* for. Money is *not* for the purchase of cars, because cars in turn *cost* money. The bus will do for now is what you should be thinking!"

I couldn't fault his logic, but I wondered where he was ultimately going with this theme since once I had the money in my mitts what could he do about it?

"You must *think* before letting money go, you must *think* and stop yourself *before you act*. Money can't be spent; money can't be touched; money is a finite and precious resource and must be used like magic dust. You see," he pointed out, "a butterfly can only *fly* if it has magic dust on its wings. Take away that magic dust and the butterfly is grounded. Your business is a butterfly, if you lose your magic dust it will never get off the ground!"

I followed his butterfly metaphor but had to say to myself that I thought it got silly at the magic dust part. I did though hear him out patiently on the principle that, at the end of the financial-stroke-natural history lesson, there would still be a whopping *five grand* in my account burning an oxyacetylene hole in my pocket. We parted with my solemn promise to use the bank's money wisely and consult faithfully each and every time I planned to withdraw more than one hundred and fifty quid.

My first purchase was a car.

The unassailable logic behind this was that Mr A Bandon (his name really couldn't have been less indicative of his nature!) had clearly meant (when talking about not buying cars) not to buy a *new* car, which of course would have been crazy. *This* car was a cheap old wreck, and on this basis you couldn't fault it. It was a green bull-nosed Saab, cost me sixty-five quid, and ran like a dream. Not only this but as the guy who sold it to me pointed out, *these cars run forever, and hardly ever go wrong.*

This, I thought wryly, must be the exception that proves the rule, after repairs in the first week cost me a further two hundred quid. But now it ran *sweet as a nut,* the mechanic ambitiously suggested when handing back the keys. *Fucking mechanics* I cursed inwardly. They cause more problems than they solve! After another two hundred though he had it going *really well,* and I felt ready to do business. My father was *most seriously displeased* (quote unquote) with my recent spending, but surely it's well known that every young man must have *wheels* or his business brain simply doesn't function? It wasn't a great start though, since the franchise needed a multi-tasking genius who required no sleep. Discovering this early on, I wondered why everyone raved about starting their own business. It must have been the Marquis de Sade, who, having suffered torments by starting up in a *small way* himself, pushed out this notion that franchises are a good idea and sat back laughing at the results. In the meantime poor saps like me screamed in eternal agony trying to run them. It took all day to sell the product, and all night to work out how much you had lost. No fun. However, after a while, just as you eventually got used to sticking needles in your eyes, it began not to seem so bad. Things picked up in fact, and I nearly enjoyed the week marked *35* in my diary. I thought about the business all the time now, and realised that I was living and breathing it and more, and that I was actually enjoying it! In time devoted to *planning ahead,* I read a few trade journals about franchising, and thought that my fledgling business could actually, with head held high, join a professional association. This was a big leap into the unknown of course, but it would be interesting. I looked to see if there was any professional representation for franchising in Castletown. Yes, in River Row there was an office of Franchise People. After making enquiries by 'phone, I booked myself into meet a Ms Ropey at 11 a.m. sharp the next morning.

The Franchise People, Franchise Association was housed in a building that it shared with a number of other firms. Among the names on the large stainless steel plaque I noticed Castletown Conservatives, and Castletown Enterprise Group. I had ascended to the third floor foyer, and was still scanning the board when a face I recognised as the sweaty Mr Wake from *Indian Joes,* interrupted my perusal. I would have loved to avoid him obviously, but things went against me when he turned directly to me.

"Ah ... hello! I understand you're here to see Ms Ropey?"

I wondered how he knew this, but then I was, perhaps, just beginning to see how things *worked* in this town. It was indeed a town with *knobs on* as well as *(k)nobs in.* He read my face and smiled knowingly. "Small town, small town."

With this he sheared off to speak to another *small-town* being. The two *got talking,* looking over at me every so often with shared half-smiles. Ms Ropey came out in due course and introduced herself as the Castletown Franchise People, Franchise Director. She had on sensible shoes and suit. In all regards she seemed normal enough. The only catch was, I couldn't tell if she was talking to me or the building across the road, since she had a squint so profound that she looked as if she lived in the world at the back of her own eyes, where she saw only her eye-sockets from the wrong way round. She continued, as I sought to adjust to the weirdness of this non-encounter asking if I'd *like to come up to the conference room to meet the rest of the team.*

I said that I would, thankful to escape from the trap of my own awkwardness. Although a little disconcerted by the *not-looking-anywhere-in-particular* Ms Ropey, I was nonetheless keen to make a good impression. It was a small conference room and we all looked forward to a very close encounter during the meeting. There was though, to be a ten-minute delay before *kick-off* it turned out, owing to a couple of latecomers. Thus, I was able to let my gaze dwell on the various characteristics of other delegates, playing a game of *who's who* in my own mind while we waited. Ms Ropey was known, so I put her first on the list. As Castletown Franchise People, Franchise Director, she was probably the most senior personage there. After her, and sitting next to her was, I guessed, her secretary or assistant – a dreamy looking woman in a cream two-piece suit. I chalked her up as a possible ally and mother-figure for my boyish charms to exploit if required. Further along there was an older man with silvering hair, who was, most likely, the chairman I guessed. Then there were two younger ones, a man and woman, as *a pair* (they may also have been *together* – *together* as well but certainly in the same business at the meeting) who were much the same age as me I thought – around twenty-five or so. Then there was a matronly woman in her fifties, wearing expensive clothes and over much good quality scent. She, I said to myself, is a businesswoman who has *made it under her own steam.* Not from looks obviously, but from having a good brain, common sense and good judgement. Suddenly the meeting got going as the stragglers arrived with apologies and uninteresting explanations. The game I had been playing turned out to be largely accurate, except for the older gentleman who was in reality, the *big boss* from the Franchise Association's HQ in London. This oversaw all the local associations' practices and quality control. Ms Ropey started the proceedings off though, paying immediate homage to Mr Languine, he from HQ with silvering hair. She spoke about him but looked very eagerly at the water cooler. She then started on the objectives of the meeting and what would be *under consideration today.*

It turned out, rather disquietingly, that getting into the Association was not just a quick form filling exercise and an annual fee. Not great news, since the rumour was being put about as I sat there by Ropey, that they had to look *in careful detail* at each separate application, *on its merits* and in terms of the *background and suitability* of the applicant/s. I was less than chuffed at the last part. Ever since I could recall, life threw this *googly* of *suitability* at you without prior warning. It would be okay if you could have pinned it down a bit more. The issue was that the goalposts were moving around like chess pieces. One day you had to have just this thing. Then the next you needed this, plus this and this. Today I may be required to have a character reference signed personally by the Pope saying what a good bloke I was. They could make this stuff up as they went along. Ropey had made it clear in the *intro* that we were to be *looked into* as suitable additions to the Franchise People, Franchise Association, and could expect to be questioned on our *probity* and *business ethics.* It was like an unannounced exam from your teacher with subjects you didn't even recognise. You would know if you had passed or failed at the end. The only sliver of good news was that it would be the turn of the two smartly dressed (about my age, maybe *together-together* but certainly together as a business duo) first. I consoled myself that at least I would get a look at how the whole thing worked before it was my *turn*. They were disconcertingly slick and good. They were already prepared with notes and reasons why they would be good additions to the association and what they could *bring to the role*. I was beginning to really work up a healthy dislike for them both by the time it was my *turn*. I hadn't been up against an ordeal like this for some time, but I was determined to do my best. In the end they *actually* let me in. I was quite surprised but it really *was the case*. After a period of reflection when the candidates under consideration had to "sit out" they came down on the side of letting us all in, on condition that we abided by the rules of the Association, and bunged them £150 quid for the privilege yearly. I was, despite the parting of money for the annual fee, damned happy to be accepted. It was almost as though I had become a fully decorated member of Castletown itself. I wasn't yet a Big (K)nob of course, but it was a start.

I walked back to my digs in a good mood. The landlord was there to meet me on the front step.

"You've gotta move out," my landlord greeted me cheerily."

I could have spent time wondering where the art of preamble and small talk had gone, but just settled for: "Why?"

"They're redeveloping the site, and I want you and the other hippies out by the beginning of next month."

At least he put things simply, making off directly into his own "area" of the building, making himself unavailable for further comment. He did though send round an ungrammatical note the next day to all the "bed-sits" in the large Victorian house that I had fondly called my "bastard digs" for the past two years. It read very much as he had indicated the day before. "All tenants will have to be vacating their rooms since we, his company name, have been acquired by another company name, which will be redeveloping this site as of (giving the date as three weeks later).

It was still at a time when they could do this kind of thing and we all obliged by buggering off pretty smart-ish in order to get good references. It was time to move up in the world to Castletown itself I decided. My business and my status demanded it and my social life would surely benefit too. I found a new place within two days because of Toni from *Indian Joes*. He was leaving his place to go back to Sicily for a "quieter life" he said. I didn't want to point out the inherent contradiction in this in case he changed his mind, saying I would take it straight away. I paid the rest of my rent off (I was on a weekly rent book at the time) and moved in over the following weekend and started my new life in Castletown proper. I felt exhilarated to be in the centre of town. The attractions were obvious to any young man.

You could:

a) Get drunk and still stagger, usually reliably, straight home where longer staggers are far more unpredictable.

b) Find yourself a girl to "get into bed" with the hope that (because it was such a short walk) she wouldn't have changed her mind by the time you got her there.

c) Go out to eat and still get back in time to pick up the wallet you've forgotten at home before the restaurant called the police.

d) Play music as loud as you liked and not be "found out" because everybody is making exactly the same kind of racket.

It was, I have to admit in hindsight, a young man's thing though. The thought of being in the middle of that kind of noise now is not pretty. This story is about *that time* though, and I loved every minute of it. Toni had left me thirty beers at a knockdown price since he couldn't take them back to Italy and because he had stolen them from *Indian Joes*. It was a great deal and meant I didn't have that expense of buying any more for the first month as my infant business continued to grow. All was rosy.

Thus it was a jolt of a highly unpleasant kind that I got next. The court case, "Wavegate" if you like, had been over for quite some time and really substantially out of my mind. I had a new business website (they had only just been introduced) that brought in most of my business. I had both designed and written it myself, though I needed the skills of a firm to turn it into a site proper. It had been a proud moment though when it "went live". For the limited time I had been in business it proved itself many times over. In short, it was the mainstay and shop window for the business with customers and suppliers all unanimous in praise of it. I put the success I currently enjoyed down to the site, coupled with many hours of grafting into the early hours. There were others who actually *stole* information from my site, changed it slightly, and put it up on their own sites. I was quite indulgent in my attitude to this, seeing it as a compliment more than anything else. I was absolutely astonished therefore when I discovered, linked to my name, and on the very same page as my site, an online diary (or "blog" as we now call them) savaging me, my name and my business with obscenities and lies. Someone, whoever this character was, had made my company logo into a parody of the royal crest. The lion and the unicorn both bore my face. My company logo was a ghastly parody of my own, sticking two fingers up in the direction of the reader in the form of a *Royal Wave*. The content of this *blog* was even worse. The guy (he called himself *Mr Shortbread*) was *on my case*, with revelations in his diary (blog) about me, and what I had been *up to* he said. He used language such as *the icing on the rancid cake* and *the poison cherry on top*. He talked about the Candid debacle as though it was happening all over again, giving his readers ideas about how to make sure that my birdseed franchise never made it *off the blocks*. *Mr Shortbread* also gave a description of what the franchise was, where I was living, and urged others to attack me in ways that could *not be traced*. He set it out as though they were hounds on the scent of blood – my blood. He had already roused an ugly mob by the looks of it. There were others on the blog with far-fetched names. There was *Miss Breadstick, Jammy-Dodger* and *Billy Battenberg.* These were already *in the know* it seemed about me and my villainous past. A whole subculture had grown up around me and this re-concocted past like slime round a pond. Inhuman pond-life from the *web* was multiplying in a feeding frenzy for flesh. Flesh-eating pond-life having come to life, harboured a death wish for yours truly and everything I stood for. It was unappetising reading for me and I spent a long night tracking the roots of this cancerous growth in all its tendrils and strands as they split off to other *sites, blogs, comments* and *links.* The *search engine,* like an enormous power-mad ghoul had given the worst tendencies in human nature mind-blowing powers of destruction over other human beings' rights to exist. It had set burning a chain of flesh-eating among countless other poison *bloggers,* wearing a thin veil labelled *free speech.* The embodiment of *Free Speech* was in truth a wanton strumpet whose defiled behaviour ran unchecked among her and her many sick *lovers.* She mocked people's misery, *cooing* about the *right to speak out,* and *the truth, the truth, the truth...*

Yeah, *fuck off love,* I thought, *the truth according to whom?*

Ah yes, of course! The truth according to the *Goo Ghoul,* I said to myself. Whatever its proclaimed merits as a means of accessing information, it remains (at least among some) an unaccountable, unstoppable, multi-headed monster of subversion and hatred. Its liberty to expel any amount of lying into the world denies others their lives. On this battlefield no rules apply and no geography exists. Myself, and others like me, are like soldiers sent into battle without armour or weapons. Maps are of no use either, because there is no territory to see. Like threads of smoke, the enemy defies capture and censure. This battle is fought according to The *Law of the Goo-Ghoul* – a massive obscene *weather system of shadenfreude*. May it die horribly and soon, I thought without hope.

Chunk Thirteen.

Loose Cannons

Since the kerfuffle of the recent US bombings it had been much quieter here in Castletown. The Americans don't like being abroad when there are troubles at home. It had been through a very long period of insularity even so I thought. It was all bad for business. I had recently, in a small way, taken an initiative with a salesman to sell my product. He was called *Smelly Dudley* to his friends and intimates, and seemed amiable enough. His best asset was being very hard working and highly subservient. I had him down, I must admit, as a bit of a loser, in character somewhere between Golem and Uriah Heep. He was ingratiating and anxious to please. It was sometimes a case of shaking him off like an old sticking plaster that just won't detach. He did his job well enough though and I tolerated him. I had no idea when I took him on just how dodgy he really was. He would, perhaps, have been okay on his own, but he had a mad wife who turned out to be part of the *deal*. If I had been aware of this I would never have gone into it I told myself afterwards. But he did. She was mad and she was bad – she was also (it turned out) dangerous to know! Things in these recession-hit days have taken a turn downward in the business. I have been looking around for new markets and to squeeze a little extra out of my margins. To this end *Smelly Dudley*, who it was that I was using, seemed to know what he was doing.

"How come you're so fat, Dud?" I put to him one time in a spirit of friendly inquiry.

"Bodybuilding!" He came back with.

I looked surprised.

"No really," he continued, countering my sceptical look. "If you body-build like me and don't keep it up, all your muscle *turns to fat*."

"So you didn't just eat all the pies then?"

He looked a trifle offended at this, and said that he viewed himself as *sturdy*. I suspected there was a mother in the background selling him this fiction but left it. After all, his having eaten the pies in a sturdy kind of way was his business. He continued to do what he did moderately well until he unleashed his mad wife onto the scene. His mad wife was called Emmanuelle – she was French. French and mad. It wasn't long until the – until then invisible – *thread-veins* of her madness started to stand out in our lives. She would, for example phone Dud up about twenty times a day at work to ask if he was alone. I thought this a stupid enough question, considering that he was working with me, but she kept calling him to ask it. Yet more irritatingly when Dud wasn't around she called me to see if:

1.   He was around, which he sometimes wasn't.

2.   Whether although he wasn't around, would he have been alone if he had been there? This was too surreal for me at 8.30 in the morning.

Also,

3.   Could he call her the moment he got into say if he would be alone for the rest of the day or not?

We carried on like this for some months until she progressed in her nuttyfication. We were soon receiving calls for Dud at the weekend when he would have been at home, and if he wasn't he certainly wasn't at work. Emmanuelle was a darker shade of nut (nutty if you will) brown, and quite curvy when she first appeared on the scene, but now she had become anorexic and pale. Her mind, by contrast, was dark and it cast its shadow over Smelly Dud. He became ever more secretive and difficult to talk to.

The business started ailing.

It all came to a head when the bailiffs dropped by for a friendly chat and a cup of tea. It was about an unpaid bill for the business rates from Castletown Council, who were of the opinion that the business owed them money. They had a firm of bailiffs, who to give them due, were a couple of big blokes in matching suits and faces of brutal simplicity. They were just right for the job I thought, mixing a strong odour of physical threat with an ability to say only one thing – to wit:

"You owe the council money and we've come to collect it."

Keeping it simple is always best in matters of cash I think. The moment you get onto any other subject you are really just getting away from your goal. These guys stuck to basics. They stood about seven foot tall, got in the way of comings and goings, and made life pretty hairy until you paid them. The problem, eternally a problem I guess, is that money is not always available for collection by the bailiff service, and explaining this can sometimes be challenging.

Dud was in the office on the fateful day the two big friendly guys referred to above came to see us for the business rates. They introduced themselves as Mick and Mike. They looked a little like the Blues Brothers with an English twist. They came in on a foot-in-the-door basis much beloved of bailiffs and the like. I was impressed by their building entering skills.

Chunk Fourteen.

(Very) Telling Tales

Ms Ropey was becoming a pain. She was a person who liked to make things up as she went along. It could be a good quality I thought in a *working girl,* but not in a bulldog-like businesswoman with flat shoes and a horrific squint. Her notion of running the Franchise People, Franchise Association was that of a monarch exercising royal prerogative, and I considered it ironic that she should be the crowned *Pit-bull Queen* of her own sub-kingdom of Castletown. We had, despite my inadvertent slur on her good name, a very good Royal already, doing a great job, thank you very much! *Pit-bull Queen* was imperious too; this came out at the second meeting I attended of the Franchise People, Franchise Association. She pounced on me at the start with:

"The rules of the Franchise People, Franchise Association quite clearly state that you must put the Association logo on your headed paper – as yet this is something you have not done ... We would not wish to sever our connections with you so soon after you have joined."

She was severe. She delivered all of this with a meaningful look, before turning away to talk to someone else before I could defend myself. The word *sever* when delivered imperiously by *queens* always makes one gulp I find! These were days when you couldn't just press a button and produce your own printing from nowhere. It was part of a *learning curve* to get things like headed paper done, and all the other touches that make running your own business. Ropey was to become a tyrant-queen on things like this especially if you didn't *jump to it*. It also came as a shock to discover that she and the *Silvering One* were actually bedfellows. It put the whole notion of *association* in the Franchise Association on a new footing I thought. They were effectively *king and queen* of the national and the regional Franchise People, Franchise Association reigning united and supreme – the *Ferdinand and Isabella* of franchise. I wondered to myself if their *pillow talk* included discussions about the – possibly superfluous – riffraff they'd invited into the Association (naming no names) like me for example. It wouldn't be long either until I received a further warning shot across the bows. The next meeting was a month later and I'd managed to get the Association's logo up on my letterhead, and felt pleased with myself. When I came face to double-face with the boss-eyed boss, and her silver-plated lover, I felt pretty confident. I gleefully exposed the franchise letterhead and smiled broadly. She however, giving the pot plant a disparaging look, pointed out to me, or perhaps it was intended for the *exit sign*, that *yes*, I had indeed complied with this, but that I had *failed to obtain permission from the Association, in writing* to *use* the official logo, which was stated *perfectly clearly* in the franchise guidelines. I thought this was a petty technicality and I told her so. To this she countered that *all members either adhered to procedure or were entirely welcome to leave.*

She was highly peeked I could tell. I decided to leave it and sit down in a warmer part of the room. I got the sympathetic eye of the cream-suited woman (Maureen) who I was counting on in the first meeting and thought that at *tea and biscuits* time I would talk to her about this.

When the moment arrived Maureen was friendly and helpful.

"You'll have to be on your guard if you want the Association to work for you. Ms Ropey can be a *very difficult woman.* I think she must have suffered at school because of, well ... (she whispered this) *you know what.*"

I looked over at the subject of our whispered exchanges and saw Ropey talking to the filing cabinet, or possibly the fire alarm.

"Oh yes, I see what you mean, but do I really have to get permission in writing to use the logo, given that I have already been accepted by the Association and paid my fees?"

"It sort of depends on *who you are and how you approach her*. If she's in a good mood, or she warms to you, pretty much anything goes. Cross her and you're *out in the cold*."

I took the advice seriously. Maureen was nice and looked kindly upon me, but I was also young and obstinate, rebellious etc. I would see, I told myself, what I could *get away with*, while staying within the rules – just. It didn't take me long to attract further censure. I had noticed there was a connection of some sort between the Franchise Association and the poison blog that was attacking me on the web. It must be someone in the meetings I thought, or someone who has *the ear* of someone attending the meetings. I was paranoid about this when I went back to the next meeting the following month. We discussed all the usual dross that meetings were made up of. Then we waited while various cliques decided what we should do with the *Contingency Advertising Budget*. I had decided very clearly for myself that my first flush of excitement and pleasure at being part of this trade association was wearing off in a big way. I had observed a very disturbing trend in the behaviour of cliques and clubs and determined that when this flirtation was over, I wouldn't be joining any more. I wasn't a club-joiner I decided. Whereas the playground antics of the characters in the Franchise Association *club* were enough to bring my blood to a gentle simmer, the out and out puerility of *siding with so and so,* or *ganging up against such and such* that went on, was of blood-boiling calibre. I thought probably that the best solution was to obtain the services of a local axe-murderer prepared to do a bit of *moonlighting*. I would be lucky if this lasted long enough to make the annual fee worthwhile. I looked around me suspicious of almost everyone except Maureen. Who was this (he or she) bastard who was *shopping me* to the web-hater every time I attended one of these meetings? Ropey was on her feet now addressing either our meeting or the one taking place in the meeting room across the corridor.

"The matter of multinational chains is what you might call *the elephant in the room.*"

I liked the image (I like elephants generally) but preferred to believe that heading this menagerie was not an elephant in the room but an enormous evil-tempered rhinoceros *behind the door*. I was pretty sure it was there now, poised to gore us all to death horribly as we left. Ropey herself was not on the lookout for rhinos as it happened since, more than likely, *she was the rhino*. Or at least, if not, she had hired one from *rhinos-r-us* for the day. She continued her address to the meeting and general neighbourhood of Castletown. Ropey continued.

"What we have is the huge question of our response to multinationals moving in, muscling in, on Castletown. Castletown is not just *any* town. We have a duty to stick up for ourselves, and all the smaller operators in our franchise in this area. These multinationals are aggressive."

Yeah right, *Rhino-Woman* I thought, like you're not!

"And will stop at nothing to get what they want. They'll be on top of us before we know it! We need a plan of action.

So, can we now split into small groups for discussion of such a plan and reconvene generally in three quarters of an hour? Thank you."

I looked about me for a place to escape but found only the smart young – possibly a couple – business couple eyeing me up as a possible collaborator at the younger end of the Association. I gave into their attentions and let them do the talking; since this was evidently the way they wanted it.

Female Business-Partner (FBP) started up. "We feel, strongly that we should stand up for the small people."

Male Business Partner (MBP), unsurprisingly, agreed with her. "We shouldn't be trodden on."

He was thinking of the *rhino* too I concluded. As I didn't want to add anything, I looked ahead of me as I had done in the infamous *Court 2*. I awaited a verdict to be arrived at by this over-talkative business – possibly lovers – duo.

"We need representation, and this association needs to *up* its *game* to challenge the multinational juggernaut," FBP piped up.

"We also need strong leadership to counter the arguments of the highly paid lawyers of *fat cat* multinationals," MBP added.

They sounded very well informed and slick I must admit, and since I didn't really have much to add I just continued to stare ahead and listen. They put forward a plan to present to old Ropey, featuring an advertising initiative with, broadly, *small is beautiful* as the theme. It would carry the Castletown image of a castle and a river, and feature in all the tourist literature and in all franchise members' premises. They had a bullet-point list of actions to *action* and suggestions to suggest. I would stick with them I thought, probably getting some cache from the connection with Ropey, and be back on snarling-terms in no time. The time came for Ropey to re-take the stand to do a bit of ad hoc sorting of wheat (business duo) from chaff (me). Since I had cunningly linked myself like a spare molecule to this high calibre *formula* of talent, I was quietly confident. She scanned the room as best she could while all the while looking at the inside of her head, settling (she had a nose for blood) on us.

"Well, why don't you three youngsters come up and tell us what to do?"

She issued this challenge with the body language of the aforementioned rancorous *rhino*, keen not to waste any time in getting behind the door should our efforts fall short of the mark. We all traipsed up to the front. Or perhaps I traipsed and the business-duo strode. We made an odd team with business-duo *fused* to each other like a barbeque accident, and me, way off to one side, like a very dubious *graft*. It looked pretty funny, but Ropey seemed to be snorting and pawing the ground in a soured herbivore kind of way I noted. It would be interesting to see what the *floor* made of the suggestions, and if the consensus was for cheering or goring. I held my breath and my tongue as the *dynamic-business-duo* started to *work the crowd*. They were pretty impressive. Ropey clearly was in a quandary over whether to *pick on me* individually. I held my breath. Then suddenly the presentation was over; inexplicably I had been spared from her talons as an overfed vulture might eventually disdain further flesh. I assumed she was keeping her *powder dry* for more favourable feeding conditions. All the various franchisees had their *go* at putting forward plans for offsetting the effects of large greedy firms taking over in Castletown. They put forward proposals that would (they hoped) ensure small greedy firms got a greater *share of the action.* We had settled on an advertising campaign to be *rolled out* over the coming months. The meeting concluded and it was time to get away. I for one edged carefully past the door where the *rhino* was.

Part Fifteen.

Castellated Pillocks of the Community

Castletown was, and is, not just any town, as we know. *Pomp and ceremony* were constant ingredients in the life of the town and in the makeup of the folk. It was no surprise then that the local Arts Centre had an initiative to promote the biggest (k)nobs in Castletown, via a *bash* soon to occur dubbed *Castletown's Top 100.* The notion of a set of the 100 most significant people, the most important people in a town, was pretty vulgar even for Castletown (a town with (K)nobs on, and in). It was *pushing the envelope* of self-importance beyond the usual boundaries of pompousness. But it was happening. Castletown's *Top 100* people were to be honoured and appreciated. They would be depicted in a number of ways. They would be pictured in places in the town where people went, doctors' surgeries, the hideous Council Offices, the Guildhall, newsagents' etc. There was also to be an event at the Castletown Arts Centre in honour of these *special* people on May 26th, a Friday evening, *7.30 p.m. for 8 o'clock*. I thought it might be nice to go along and see who they were, so I could abase myself on future occasions if I met any of them socially. The event was titled *Castletown's Top 100* an evening *to honour the best of our town*. Ricky Buffool would compare it, a TV comic actor turned local celebrity. He would introduce each of *the 100*, giving a quick synopsis of why they were such *top people*, rallying the rest of the audience, all also in the *Top 100* themselves, to applaud and cheer. Nobody *not* in the *Top 100 People* would be invited, or allowed into the auditorium, though they could still use the bar. It would be great backslapping, self-congratulatory pompous evening for the town. I was really looking forward to it.

Meantime, in the running of my precarious business, I was still getting *fan mail* from *well-wishers* on the Web. They'd formed themselves into an ugly mob of vengeful pitchfork brandishers and torch wavers. They were every inch the lewd, cackling degenerates of countless generations; the ugly mob of Hammer Horror Films. In the *here and now* they were a pestilence afflicting the modern medium of the Internet. They were though, exactly the same ugly mob, the same ugly modern-medieval minds, baying for blood. Their noses, always *on the scent* of weakness, they crept along the sewer of the Web. It was time to think of something else.

The event at Castletown Arts Centre was later today I noted – the morning of Friday, May 26th. I was looking forward to watching the *Top 100 Castletowners* pile into the Arts Centre from the safety of the bar, waiting to see who was who in the upper strata of Castletown society. I got there early and ordered a Whiskey Sour. It was my favourite drink at the time. Who was to be *King of the Castle* I wondered, or *Queen* of course. Certainly I knew who the *Dirty Rascal* was! When you get *100 Top People* together, human nature dictates there still needs to be just one *Supreme Being*, right? There has to be a *top of the top*. The rest would be merely *top* – not *the top*.

Castletown's *Top People* started arriving at approximately 6.30 p.m. I say approximately because I was getting a little *the worse for wear* as the expression goes. I was drinking on an empty stomach and really enjoying it – too much so to heed the warning signs. Others may have noticed them I think. I was getting distracted trying to guess who would *be there*. This *guessing game* was a variant of my franchise meeting game of guessing *who's who*. In this game you didn't have anyone in front of you, but enjoyed images of those figures in the *Castletown Club* who you thought were bound to be there. The thing was, if some of the people I was thinking of had *not* been invited, a mass nose re-jointing exercise would be needed and quick! I pondered on this as a few figures arrived, and was disappointed to find that I didn't recognise any of them. It was easily half-an-hour until I saw my first recognisable Castletown *face*. This was *Quivering Woman* herself and she was *dressed to impress*. The amount of quivering she was doing far out-stripped her performance at work. She was like a jelly in a high wind, shaking and billowing with self-importance. In she went while I looked around for more faces I knew. I saw nobody else under this heading until the Council Leader and Head of Planning turned up like the *Gruesome Twosome* of *Wacky Races* fame, along with various others from Castletown Council. They were joined by the innumerable other Departments including Trading Standards I noted, to include my twin-nemesis (or is it nemeses) of *Number One* and *Spidery Woman*. They all piled in together giving support to the principle of *it's who you know not what you know...* etc. I mean to say it was a bit of a coincidence otherwise that *all* of them were quite so important, right? The next clutch of celebrated ones was again unknown to me, and it was this way until Mr *Sweaty Quake* came in, and not long after him, Ms Ropey, sans *rhino*. I was really pretty drunk by now and getting ever so slightly sarcastic in my manner at this influx of the *Chosen Many*. A *chosen few*, I argued, wouldn't *influx* anyway; it was a contradiction in terms. It was a foregone thing that I would *say* something to someone in the end, I just didn't know what or to whom. The chosen *One Hundred Top People,* when viewed through the perfect lens of Whiskey Sours, were simply a gaggle of mediocre, pompous arses. Moreover, the drinks were making them look pompous-er and more arse-like all the time. They strutted about, or they swept about, conscious of their own importance, recognising the – lesser – importance of others, or rejecting it utterly by turns. It was always bound to happen I suppose and you could almost not blame them for it, given the title of the event. But then you had to of course. Only by being self-important over a sustained period would you have qualified for this contest. So yes they had to be blamed. They had to be told too, I decided. I had *paced myself* by drinking as fast and as steadily as I had been doing all night. *Pacing myself* was in this case *defined by* getting as drunk as possible as fast as possible, in order to deliver my views to my audience, who were also too drunk to feel the full, toe-curling effects of what I had to say. I went up to the large lady and gentleman on the door, sort of high-class bouncers. She also had her own pair of high-class *bouncers* I noticed, so in admiration, I started with her, keeping my speech short and clipped to avoid slurring. I had become quite good at this and I thought she might not suspect.

"John's here," I clipped.

The effect was instant and remarkable. Both the upper-crust bouncers immediately rushed past me and out through the double-doors of the Arts Centre. I was surprised by this, even in my state of whiskey-soured-ness, and ambled into the auditorium to view the amassed *chosen* folk. I walked onto the small dais that had been set up for these *pomping* ceremonies and started off with an intro to Castletown.

"Dear *chosen few*," I intoned. "Gosh aren't there are a lot of you! I want to say what an honour it is to be here tonight."

A *few* of the *chosen few* looked at me indulgently and most were still talking to others about themselves.

"I feel more than qualified," I continued as clippedly as I could manage, "... to talk to you about how important you all are, erm to um ... Castletown."

With the magic word *Castletown,* I had their attention to a man/woman now, and the response was pretty appreciative I was thinking. They looked at each other with glances of mutual self-congratulation and justly-felt pride.

"I have met some of you before," I continued, "...and I can say that I would *never have believed* the measure of regard in which you are held by this town, of all towns!"

They liked this statement. A few gurgles of pleasure percolated around the crowd like syrupy coffee. It was then I spotted Ropey and making up a sour-looking duo at the front. It immediately made my speech a little odd.

I began slurring some words, which caused a ripple effect of murmurs in the crowd, who began looking at each other questioningly. So I speeded up. "Ye*sh,* I have seen you all around in thi*ssh* great town and in some ca*shhes,* even done busin*isshh* with you. *I know you!*"

I went on enthusiastically. I was unaware of the distinct disquiet coming over the assembled *chosen few.*

"I would like to *shhay, thissh* ..." I slurred spectacularly,

"... that it eerr *ishh* ... a *real HORROR* to stare at you ... no, no, *sshorry* ... I mean an *honour, to SHARE* with you *thissh* night, your most important of all night*shh,* eerr ... eerr ... *of!*" I ended, but to me, it didn't sound quite right at the end here I thought – but there it was.

"No, no, wait, *sshorry* again, I mean to *ssshhare* a night *shho impotent* to you all! N*o!* Damn. Wrong again ... *shho* im**por**tant to you, nay ... (I let out a sharp whinny here as it seemed to fit together semantically) to Ca*shhhtletown!* I mean *you're all shhoo pompous* aren't you? Erm, by this I mean you're *rightly* pomp*ushh,* or maybe just proud per-hap*ssssshh.*" People began to look for security, which they were gratified to see had arrived and were heading my way, though severely inhibited in their progress by the *Top 100 great and good.*

"Well, I for one …" I paused for thought, "… for one … oh yes, for *one or two* … eerr drink*sshs*! Or maybe a few more … That's it! Where are the drink*sshs* by the way?? Eerr *sshorry again!* … I lost my thread for a moment there, what I *mean ishhh* … I want to *stick it up you!*"

I went on, "… no, no I what I wanted to *shayyy,* issh I want to, to … *stick it to you,* no, no, no!" I scolded myself, … to stick up *for you.*"

I had maybe half a minute to go, I continued, "… *becoshhh* … Cash*hhtletown* pom*pushh* ar*shhhes are better than any other*s! … *you can forget* pom*pushh* ar*shhhes from anywhere elssh!*"

I swept my hand impressively across the room as I pronounced on this. "Here in Cash*hhtletown* we do the *besssht* pom*pushh* …"

I think I nearly lost my thread here, but rallied. "Look!" I reasoned, I looked round to see if I could find what I was looking for myself, I couldn't, so I moved on. "Look! If ever … If ever I *shhaw* a group of people more deserving than you lot, I don't know where they are! I mean, do you??"

Again I decided to look, panning a wide angle with my hand in the same motion, around me to see if indeed I could see such a group – again I couldn't, so I continued … "I *esshpesshhly* want to pay tribute, on this*shh shhh-pesshal* evening, to the large and vigour*ushh* ARTHRITIC community … *eerr I mean ARTISHHTIC* community, erm … here in this*shh* great town!

"You! ... *Yeshh* ... *you,* have *shhpread ART* (I looked meaningfully at the *rhino in the room* (spelling out each letter, since I wasn't confident I still had them all in the palm of my hand so to speak) ... T.A.R.T!" I shouted triumphantly. "Oops, one too many T's in there, *sshorry* about that! Anyway (I collected myself) *ashh* I was *shaying* you, have *shhpread ART* ... around in this town like ... like ... the fertili*shhher* on the land that we can all detect so often hereabout*shhh*. You! You (I pointed at people individually – *QW* and *Number One* included), are such *artishhhtic shhhouls! Thish* is why I want to say thank*shhh* to you!"

Security was now really homing in on me ...

"*You* ..." I repeated myself in a last gasped spirit of conspiratorial reportage, "are all truly, truly *artishhhtic shhhouls. If ever* there was a collection of *complete and utter art-shhhouls you are it*, eerr *them*, eerr *they*!"

Here they got me. I went out happily though, with a beefy security guard under each arm. The rest was a blur until the next morning, or in truth, afternoon, when I woke up at my digs.

Chunk Sixteen.

Getting Away Chaste

I was happy to be there then and equally happy now, as I sit at my desk, recording the eventful past here in the modern-ancient town of Castletown. I have been through a lot I thought but here I am nonetheless, and still keen to go abroad into the streets and see what the folk are doing as they pursue their lives. Now as then, I walk down to the river to see the ducks. They were clearly relatives of the depressive ones that I'd seen there in a previous life because they were huddled together in a *group float,* commiserating with each other over some sadness or other. Maybe it was the quality of bread these days, or the large increase in peddle boats driven through their rushy domain by insensitive tourists. Anyway with the passage of time (and maybe through the use of foul counselling of some kind) they seemed to cheer up a little when I was down again with food. After some weeks of my attentions they got into much better spirits than their forbears. Especially *Ducky* – I recommend you go down there and see him. Take a look at Castletown's all-seeing castle and then wander down to feed the ducks and swans, taking only superior bread. As I say look out for *Ducky*, he's unmistakable. You'll notice that, nowadays even though he can look melancholy and has a far-away look in his eyes, he perks up when you call his name. Do it, seriously, it's worth it.

In the uneventful days following the Top 100 incident, I had time and leisure to observe more of the *dramatis personae* in the Castletown *play.* What of these Castletowners then? What had we learned about them? Were they the same as everyone, but with (k)nobs on? Well, yes of course they were. They didn't all have (k)nobs on either. The idea that one town is hermetically sealed from another is nonsense, just as you can't stop the air passing from one place to another, or racism or fascism passing from one mind to another. It is *in the nature of things*, as are kindness and wisdom. Castletown was just like any other town, full of people of a generally similar kind, modern yet primitive. For every Bloated Fascist, Acid Green Witch in one town, there are other examples, with different names, in other towns. They may have different names in other towns, a world away perhaps, but they are the same people. There too, you will find the kindly people like Ron, Lin and Jane from the unit where I did my community service. They were the silver lining in clouds like *Judge Grudge*, *Ropey*, *Number One* and *Spidery*. Then there was the whole legal chain of being from Updyke to Vyle, in fancy dress and plain minds. The law mongers dispensed the same *cuts* of justice, day in day out, with a nod and a wink to their fellow tradesmen. The Lins of the – outside Castletown – world carried on being an unassuming *foil* to the *Top 100 Castletowners* and their pomping-fests. Ron and his wife were *up the road a way*, living out their lives with quiet dignity (keeping*) the noiseless tenor of their way, as the poet has it*. While QW was quivering with ill-concealed self-importance, others were just *getting on with it I* thought. Actually just like the Royal who I had seen the other day close up. She had far more in common with Ron or Lin, unassuming in her own way. Good on her I thought to myself. It's the middle section that really gets up your nose – either end is okay.

I went back to the river with superior bread. The ducks et al were clearly saying to each other, *yes this is the guy my*

grandmother was always telling me about, good bread and very sympathetic to your average downtrodden waterfowl this guy. I gave them ten minutes of therapy and then sauntered off towards the Castle. It was the same old Castle that looked down imperiously (but now I reckoned) *kindly* too. It had never lost the *common touch* I thought. It kept a distant but all-seeing interest in the minute beings under its vast, steep walls. I thought that I would see what was doing at the front porch and if there was any personages to be seen today. Maybe even the Royal herself. God bless her! I thought idly. Even though this thought *had* been idle and had passed like a vapour, from my head, it was still with a frisson of surprise that *I actually saw her there* as close as I am to you now. She was looking bored actually. I wondered why she was bored in the few seconds I was near her, before she was smuggled away by bodyguards or whoever they use. She looked as though she would rather, at that moment, not be the Royal One and would have preferred to escape into the sleepy afternoon of Castletown with a headscarf on and have an ice cream; feed the ducks and swans and go for a ride in a motorboat. It was never to be however, and there she was, and then there she wasn't. I often think about that silent exchange of looks on Castletown Castle, and speculate what she may have had to say about the town and the honest and irritating folk *under her wing.* What would she secretly have and royally thought? I went to the park that is in the middle of the old centre of the somewhat fascinating old town and sat on a low wall backing onto a graveyard for the *chosen few* of yesteryear. It was uncharacteristically quiet again.

"You're lucky you didn't end up in choky," Mick started off. I looked round.

"Hi Mick, you good?"

"Yes, got myself in with the Castle, didn't I?"

"Yeah, how?"

"Well, your invention of the *Fuck-off Fingers* as every-one calls them did me a favour."

I hadn't heard this nickname until now and I wasn't sure whether to like it or not. It was quite funny.

"What are you doing then?"

"I'm doing odd jobs at the Castle for one of the gaffers in charge of maintenance. They don't pay too well but it's the *fact* that you're working *there* if you know what I mean?"

"Yeah, I understand. Well good for you Mick. I hope it works out."

"What about you?"

"Me? Well I'm working on a book," realising, almost with surprise, that I *was* in fact *working on a book*. All these observations were in my head and just bristling to get on to the page.

"One day I'll write the damned thing."

Two Castletown kids, hearing this boast, ran past and pushed me sharply in the back by accident-on-purpose.

"You little arseholes!" I bellowed as they *hared off*.

"You think you got a way with words mate?" One shouted breathlessly back at me.

"Yes!" I shouted back. "... I've got away with words and I'm not giving them back!"

www.ingramcontent.com/pod-product-compliance
Lightning Source LLC
Chambersburg PA
CBHW051140020726
47501CB00005B/1601